HOW TO GET *SINGLE DAD NEXT DOOR TO* *FINALLY NOTICE YOU!*
by Jenny Stevens

1) Offer to take care of his baby. This should prove no hardship as you simply love children, plus it shows off your terrific maternal instincts.

2) Give him every opportunity to see your domestic side: you boil a mean bottle and can crochet a bootie in seconds flat.

3) Be sure to change out of your baby-food-splattered sweatsuit when he arrives late to pick up his baby. A pretty nightgown can work wonders after midnight.

4) Once you convince him to stay for dinner, don't let him leave until his ring is on your finger!

Dear Reader,

What makes a man a SUPER FABULOUS FATHER? In bestselling author Lindsay Longford's *Undercover Daddy*, detective Walker Ford promises to protect a little boy with his life. Even though that means an undercover marriage to the child's mother—the woman he'd always loved but could never have...until now.

Book 2 of Silhouette's cross-line continuity miniseries, DADDY KNOWS LAST, continues with *Baby in a Basket* by award-winning author Helen R. Myers. A confirmed bachelor finds a baby on his doorstep—with a note claiming the baby is his!

In Carolyn Zane's *Marriage in a Bottle,* a woman is granted seven wishes by a very mysterious, very sexy stranger. And her greatest wish is to make him her husband....

How is a woman to win over a bachelor cowboy and his three protective little cowpokes? With lots of love—in *Cowboy at the Wedding* by Karen Rose Smith, book one of her new miniseries, THE BEST MEN.

Why does Laurel suddenly want to say "I do" to the insufferable—irresistible—man who broke her heart long ago? It's all in *The Honeymoon Quest* by Dana Lindsey.

All Tip wants is to be with single dad Rob Winfield and his baby daughter, but will her past catch up with her? Don't miss *Mommy for the Moment* by Lisa Kaye Laurel.

From classic love stories to romantic comedies to emotional heart tuggers, Silhouette Romance brings you six irresistible novels this month—and every month—by six talented authors. I hope you treasure each and every one.

Regards,

Melissa Senate
Senior Editor

Please address questions and book requests to:
Silhouette Reader Service
U.S.: 3010 Walden Ave., P.O. Box 1325, Buffalo, NY 14269
Canadian: P.O. Box 609, Fort Erie, Ont. L2A 5X3

HELEN R. MYERS

Baby in a Basket

Silhouette

ROMANCE™

Published by Silhouette Books

America's Publisher of Contemporary Romance

Special thanks and acknowledgment to Helen R. Myers for her contribution to the Daddy Knows Last series.

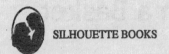 SILHOUETTE BOOKS

ISBN 0-373-19169-3

BABY IN A BASKET

Books by Helen R. Myers

HELEN R. MYERS

satisfies her preference for a reclusive life-style by living deep in the Piney Woods of East Texas with her husband, Robert, and—because they were there first—the various species of four-legged and winged creatures that wander throughout their ranch. To write has been her lifelong dream, and to bring a slightly different flavor to each book is an ongoing ambition.

Admittedly restless, she says that it helps her writing, explaining, "It makes me reach for new territory and experiment with old boundaries." In 1993, the Romance Writers of America awarded *Navarrone* the prestigious RITA for Best Short Contemporary Novel of the Year.

Meet The Soon-To-Be Moms
of New Hope, Texas!

"I'll do anything to have a baby—even if it means
going to the sperm bank. Unless sexy cowboy
Jake Spencer is willing to be a daddy...
the natural way."
—*Priscilla Barrington, hopeful mom-to-be.*

THE BABY NOTION
by Dixie Browning (Desire 7/96)

"I'm more than willing to help Mitch McCord take care
of the baby he found on his doorstep. After all, I've
been in love with that confirmed bachelor for years."
—*Jenny Stevens, maternal girl-next-door.*

BABY IN A BASKET
by Helen R. Myers (Romance 8/96)

"My soon-to-be ex-husband and I are soon-to-be
parents! Can our new arrivals also bless us with a
second chance at marriage?"
—*Valerie Kincaid, married new mom.*

MARRIED...WITH TWINS!
by Jennifer Mikels (Special Edition 9/96)

"I have vowed to be married by the time I turn thirty.
But the only man who interests me is single dad
Travis Donovan—and he doesn't know I'm alive...yet!"
—*Wendy Wilcox,
biological-clock-counting bachelorette.*

HOW TO HOOK A HUSBAND (AND A BABY)
by Carolyn Zane (Yours Truly 10/96)

"Everybody wants me to name the father of my baby.
But I can't tell anyone—even the expectant daddy!"
—*Faith Harper, prim, proper—and very pregnant.*

DISCOVERED: DADDY
by Marilyn Pappano (Intimate Moments 11/96)

Chapter One

"What a difference a day makes, eh, folks? It's Monday, August 17. Yesterday we were trying to figure out a way around our water rationing problems, and today the National Weather Service is putting us under a severe storm warning. *Ooonly* in the heat and heart of Texas! Stay right here at KDYL for breaking news about the approaching line of thunder—"

Mitch McCord shut off the radio a second before killing the 450SL's engine. He didn't need to hear anything about the weather. A different, more catastrophic storm had already exploded right over his head, and the National Weather Service would be of no use to him whatsoever. But disc jockey Ron Rowlett had said one thing worth noting: twenty-four hours could make an incredible difference in a person's life.

Amazing. Yesterday at this very moment he'd been climbing to thirty thousand feet on his way to California. Today he should be doing that again, since it was day two of his four-on, three-off flying schedule with Gulf-West Airlines. But instead of being in his 737, he was sitting here on his driveway, trying to summon the courage to go next door and face his future.

If he thought it would wake him up and put things back in sane order, he would hit his head against the steering wheel a few dozen times. Unfortunately this wasn't a dream; he was wide-awake, and the mess he found himself in didn't look like it would be going away anytime soon.

"This is your life, Captain Mitchell Sean McCord. Do not pass Go, do not collect two hundred dollars. Just get your butt out of this ego machine, and watch what the bluebird of happiness bequeaths *you.*"

To think he used to believe being grounded was the worst thing that could ever happen to him. Short of utter disaster in the sky, that is—but he worked hard not to dwell on such a thing. He was a man who stayed in control; the guy who made things happen. A participant, not an observer. Well, apparently he'd participated one time too many. Where was his infamous power of positive thinking now?

Hang gliding in the Twilight Zone.

Too true. And it did no good to sit and mope. It certainly wouldn't resolve his dilemma. Ready or not, he had to go knock at Jenny Stevens's door and say, "Hey, Jen. Guess I'd better take the kid now."

Jeez . . . he couldn't even phrase himself correctly, couldn't bring himself to think *my* kid or *my* daughter. The mere suggestion had him breaking out in a cold sweat. If he had to say the words, he would probably have a coronary. Hell, this was a fine end for someone his cohorts at the airline had dubbed "the last man with a pulse likely to marry." He sure fooled them. He'd passed the wedding ceremony entirely and gone straight into fatherhood. Man, oh, man, he wished it was Friday so he could have a drink.

A movement out of the corner of his eye had him looking toward the right where Jenny peered out at him from the lacy-curtained frame that was her kitchen window. Ever-observant Jenny. Heaven only knew what she must think of him at this point. There was a time when he'd carefully, consciously refused to let himself care what she thought. Not a nice thing to admit, but true, because she was all wrong for a guy like him. Now he needed her good heart—as badly as he needed air to breathe.

With a heavy sigh, he shoved open the door and climbed out of the sports car. There was no putting this off. If he didn't go in, she would come out. The smartest thing would be to meet her on her turf, pronounce the verdict, and beg for help. *More* help, since she'd already been wonderful this morning. Of course, he already knew what she was going to say. After living next to her for nearly half his life, he doubted Saint Jenny could surprise him much.

She would be supportive, sweetly reassuring, and generous to a suffocating fault. Agony. Nevertheless, he needed that right now—at least until he could figure out what to do about this mess.

He crossed from his property to hers, and approached the small house constructed of pink and gray granite. Red Blaze roses bloomed up the northeast wall in bubbly profusion. Red and white gladioli and pink impatiens filled the flower beds, and lace curtains framed every window. The whole place looked like something out of a fairy tale, including the white curlicue sign out front noting Jams By Jenny. The house literally oozed confectioneries and tradition. Mitch fought the urge to tug his tie loose and unbutton the collar of his shirt to keep from hyperventilating. As a rule, he avoided getting this close to Jenny's place. And it definitely went against the grain to do it twice in one day. It would be a miracle if he didn't break out in hives.

Just remember to keep the ball in your court, pal. Tell her the bad news, make your serve, and get the hell out—regardless of the outcome. All you're looking for is a temporary business arrangement.

That's it. He had to think like a professional. Every day he flew hundreds of people in a multiton jet across half a continent, then back again. Surely he could converse with one harmless female for a few minutes and come away with what he wanted.

He almost had himself convinced. Then she opened the door and laughed at him.

"Well, for pity's sake, McCord. You look like the verdict's death by hanging."

Apparently nothing was going to go as expected today. Mitch shot her a sour look. "It might as well be."

Jenny's dark eyes went wide and she clasped her hands together. "She's yours, then? I mean, of course she's yours. Anyone who looks at that baby would know it in a heartbeat. But... there's been no missing persons bulletin filed? No call by a bereft mother? What did they say at the police station? Did you stop by the hospital, as I suggested?"

Since when did the woman prattle like a teenager with her first telephone? "Let me know when it's my turn to say something."

He knew he sounded like a grump, but he simply couldn't help himself. Who needed all that bubbly chatter? And that barrage of evocative scents that attacked him as she stepped aside and he entered her kitchen! He groaned inwardly and wondered how the woman stayed so trim. Heck, even dressed in a loose print jumper, she wasn't much bigger around than the braid resting on her shoulder. Working in an environment like this, she ought to be the size of a 747!

Mitch tried not to pay too much attention to the fruit compote simmering on the stove or the just-baked muffins and breads wrapped and stacked on the counter. Jenny was almost as well-known for her baked goods as she was for her condiments. It was, however, the fresh-perked coffee that got to him the worst. At this moment he figured he could use about a potful of the stuff.

No sound came from across the room where the baby lay. This triggered Mitch's curiosity, as well as a smattering of hope. If the kid wasn't hungry at this point, Mitch told himself, he had a chance left yet, because no kid of *his* could be around aromas like this without ending up with a growling stomach. Just last Saturday while Mitch had been mowing the lawn, he about OD'd on some kind of butterscotch smell emanating from Jenny's place. But the only way he had survived was by wishing Jenny Stevens cellulite and saddlebags. The woman sure made it tough to keep to the same size uniform from season to season, let alone year after year. Heaven knows that for that thought alone, every few months he considered moving.

Suddenly a pitiful wail erupted from the woven hamper on the kitchen table. Mitch hung his head. So there it was, the final knockout punch—as if he needed one at this point.

"There, there, buttercup, we're about set."

Belatedly, Mitch noted Jenny's grandmother at the stove. She finished pouring what looked to be milk from a steaming saucepan into a glass bottle, and screwed on the nipple cap.

"What's that?" he asked as Fiona Stevens began vigorously shaking the bottle.

"A Scud missile. What's it look like?" With a roll of her big dark eyes, Fiona continued. "This is one of Jen's baby bottles—which just goes to show that you never know what's worth keeping. And inside is my own brew of sweetened milk. It's what I gave Jenny when she was a baby herself, because her mother, poor love, wasn't able to nurse her for very long." The elderly woman, who was as short and plump as Jenny was tall and slender, looked particularly proud of the job she'd done.

"Naturally." Jenny gave him a benign look. "You know *we'd* never serve anything canned or artificial. They don't call us The From Scratch Stevenses for nothing."

Ignoring Jenny's comment because he didn't have a clue as to how to reply, Mitch frowned. "Are you sure it's safe? The folks at the hospital gave me a few cans of stuff they say is the only thing I should be feeding it—I mean, her."

Fiona grunted in a way that left little doubt of her opinion of those so-called experts. "Just look at that sour face, too," she muttered to Jenny. "A walking testament to poor eating habits if I've ever seen one. I'll bet you my Julio Iglesias tape that he never tasted a drop of his own mother's breast milk in his life. Small wonder he buys into the first bit of fiddle-faddle tossed his way."

"Gran's not much into store-bought anything, unless it comes from the Baby Boutique—" Jenny interpreted with an amused look "—or carries *her* label."

Mitch decided he could care less about Fiona's buying habits. it was bad enough that the cackling old hen had little good to say to him under normal circumstances, now she was going to criticize something out of his control. Sometimes he didn't know which of the two women was worse, Jenny with her eternally sunny disposition and her eagerness to please, or Fiona, who was as blunt as a bullet.

"Could we cut the discussion of intimate body parts and try to remember there's a child present?" he told the scowling woman.

"*Now* he worries about his image." Fiona had to tilt her head way back to succeed in looking down her nose at Mitch. "Don't worry, Mr. Friendly Skies, you won't hear another word out of me. All I was saying is that this baby will know what it's like to get at least one good meal in her life."

Mitch looked from her to the basket to Jenny before rubbing his aching head. "Could we talk?" he asked Jenny. "*Alone.*"

She bit her lower lip a moment before extending her hand to the other woman whose permed and dyed hair almost matched the exterior color of the house. Her grandmother glared back with mutinous eyes the same color as her granddaughter's before slapping the bottle into Jenny's palm.

"Fine. I have to get back to my knitting machine anyway. Besides, it's almost time for my soaps."

Fiona stormed off, leaving a pained-looking Jenny, who sighed and carried the bottle to the sink, where she ran cool water over it. Not knowing what else to do,

Mitch stood there and waited. He was grateful that at least the baby had stopped crying for the moment.

"She doesn't mean to be abrasive, Mitch. It's just that despite the baby epidemic that seems to be going around New Hope, you showing up at our door with a child in your arms did come as the surprise of the century."

"How do you think *I* felt?" he muttered to the comely brunette's back.

"Mmm. I guess so. You tried to tell me before, when you asked to leave her with me, but I'm not sure I understood you correctly. You said someone left her on your front steps?"

"In that basket." As Jenny glanced over her shoulder at him, he nodded toward the table and the clothes basket, but avoided inspecting the contents again. He figured the longer he put it off, the greater the possibility that a miracle might happen. Who knows, someone could come by and say this was all a misunderstanding, that the baby was theirs—and not his.

"And there was a note attached that said 'Take care of *your* baby,'" Jenny said, finishing for him. "That's it? No signature? No indication as to what time the mother might want her back?"

"I don't think whoever did this planned to use me as a day-care center, Jen. There was nothing else on the note." Every time Mitch thought about it he kept getting an extremely weak feeling in the pit of his belly. "Who would do such a thing? It's...barbarian!"

"There must be some explanation. The mother must be in the dark about what's happened." Testing the liquid on her wrist, Jenny crossed to the table. "Come on, sweetheart." She lifted the infant carefully into her arms, and as she eased the bottle into the baby's eager, open mouth, she made a wistful sound. "How precious. Mitch, with every passing minute I'm around this child, I'm more and more convinced she must have been kidnapped. No mother could give up a gift like this. You don't have a clue as to who that person might be?"

"Do you think I'd have made a fool of myself by going to the police and the hospital, if I did? How am I supposed to guess something like that?"

After a startled glance, Jenny's expression turned wry, and she eased onto one of the dinette chairs to better support the baby. "It's elementary, Watson. You simply count back nine months, add—oh, I'd say a few days, no more—and whoever you were with in the, er, biblical sense, is more than likely your baby's mother."

Now she was going to be a comedienne? "Listen, I went through enough of that talk with Tyson down at the police station." He and Brad had gone to school together, and his friend now had two young, ferociously energetic twin boys. Brad had been all too happy to use his stature as a *legal* father to pick on Mitch. "I can count."

"Well, then . . . have you?"

He stared at Jenny's expectant face. She had skin as creamy and smooth as the sweet milk she was feeding the baby, and an honest, winsome face that while not stop-in-your-tracks stunning, was complemented by soulful eyes and a tug-at-your-heart smile. In an odd way, she had always bothered him, but she was not the kind of woman he dated, and she certainly wasn't the person with whom he should be having this conversation.

He cleared his throat. "No."

"Why not?"

Because he'd been terrified—*was* terrified. Because he still didn't want to believe this was happening to him. Because she was the last person he wanted to admit the answer to.

When he didn't reply, she nodded toward the wall by the telephone. "There's a calendar over there."

She had to be kidding? "Jen, regardless of what conclusion you've come to, I don't know that this is my baby."

"You mean the police are going to let you keep someone else's baby? And the hospital didn't insist you bring in this stranger's child so they could ensure expert care for her?" she mused, lifting her finely arched eyebrows again. "I thought you were pretty sharp to charm me into watching this little darling while you were gone for an hour or so, but to continue to avoid claiming her, while obviously convincing the authorities not to take her...wow! Your powers of persuasion are beyond even what I thought you capable of. Why, you're in a class all of your own!"

And he'd brought the child here because he believed Jenny Stevens was a pushover? A marshmallow? The eternal good samaritan who did noble deeds without being judgmental? Boy, had he been living in fantasyland. Jenny intended to find out who the mother was, and she wasn't going to let him rest until he figured it out and confessed it to her. If Saint Peter ever needed a vacation from guarding the pearly gates, Jenny Stevens would be a perfect replacement.

But despite his annoyance, Mitch's guilt was that much stronger. Once again he hung his head in shame.

"All right," Jenny said with a sigh. "What *did* Chief Tyson say?"

"Exactly what you've already guessed. I told him what happened, and he told me that if I continue to insist the baby couldn't be mine, that I need to bring her in and turn her over to him, whereupon she would become a ward of the state and go into foster care while they try to either find the biological parents or arrange for new legal ones."

"But you're not denying you're the father anymore, are you?"

Although softly posed, her question held a strong challenge, and he knew that if he answered, if he continued with his plan to ask Jenny for more help, things would never be the same again. He was at a crossroads, and while he knew the path he chose would change his life drastically, he was equally leery at how it would affect them as neighbors.

Mitch rubbed the back of his neck. "Hell, Jen. I can't talk to you about this."

"Oh, for pity's sake! I do know where babies come from and how this one was made, McCord. What's more, you look as if you need to talk to someone, or go out of your mind. Now, I may be a bit disappointed in the choices you made that ultimately resulted in your conceiving this child, but it would be a waste of good oxygen to criticize what's already written in stone. Go ahead and say what you need to say."

He should have known generous Jenny would be a pillar of logic. He liked to think he possessed his fair share, too; however, he was more successful on a subjective basis. People, especially women, who could be continually objective made him nervous. Somehow they seemed incongruous to all of his theories about the female species.

Mitch gave himself a mental shake. If Jenny wanted the truth, so be it. Maybe when inundated with a full dose, she would stop looking at him as if she expected him to pick up a lance and mount a noble charger for her. He'd never been the white knight type and didn't want to start.

Jenny watched Mitch McCord struggle with his decision. It was nothing new. She'd seen him debate over how to respond to her countless times over the years that they'd been neighbors.

She wasn't his type. Mitch was a picture-perfect image of the American heartthrob: Robert Redford good looks complemented by amber eyes guaranteed to twinkle at almost any female from seven onward, even when he wasn't smiling beneath that dark mustache. Put him in his airline uniform and he cut a devastating figure.

He was, however, equally lethal when stripped down to a pair of well-fitted jeans and sweaty from mowing his lawn. According to New Hope gossip, women melted in his presence, and he seemed to like them in return, considering the rumors that constantly floated around about him being seen with this ex-beauty queen or that wealthy divorcée. Unfortunately, Jenny had never been able to count herself among those lucky souls.

Years ago, after she'd asked him to be her escort to her senior prom, he'd made it clear that he would never date her. He'd said it was because she was his neighbor and too nice of a girl. A ''forever girl'' was how he had suavely put it, the stinker. He had that way about him, an ability to keep a girl's heart tied in knots, even if there was no hope that she would ever win his. At least he'd been circumspect over the past decade and had conducted his liaisons away from his house and out of her view. That meant a great deal to Jenny.

She had a feeling that despite what he'd said so long ago, she bothered him. Maybe she didn't have the flashy, cosmopolitan look so many women had today, but sometimes she found him watching her with a strange look in his eye. She couldn't quite define it—she doubted he could explain it himself—but she made him uncomfortable, and hesitant, restless, when they were alone.

No, she wasn't his type. But she planned to be. Someday. She believed it with the same simple and clear faith that had helped her build her modest but thriving business. The key was patience. Long ago her grandmother had taught her that a yeast bread wouldn't rise before it was ready. In the same way, Jenny believed that when the time was right, Mitch would open his eyes and realize they could be good together.

On the other hand, who said a lady couldn't turn up the heat a bit to coax things along? She watched tight-lipped Mitch as he headed for the calendar, and bowed her head over the baby to hide a satisfied smile.

Mitch flipped pages back and forth, back and forth. Beneath the jacket of his black pilot's uniform, she saw his broad shoulders stiffen and square. He knows, she thought, feeling a knot tighten in her own stomach. Would it turn out to be someone she knew? Someone she actually liked? That would be tough to handle. Maybe even dream-shattering.

"Oh, brother."

The dull mutter wasn't meant for her ears, but Jenny didn't care. "What?"

"I can't believe it."

"Mitch, I'm holding physical proof to the contrary in my arms. Would you mind telling me what conclusion you've come to over there?"

When he finally faced her, his gaze was vague, his thoughts clearly turned inward. "She would no more want to be a mother than I'm ready to be a father."

"She *who?*"

Beneath his neatly trimmed mustache, his firm mouth turned downward. "Savannah Sinclair."

Of all the people he could have mentioned! Jenny had to fight back a cry of outrage. But it was too much to ask her to be silent. "No. Oh, no, no, *no.*"

Mitch scowled back at her. "I heard you the first time."

"Then tell me you were only kidding. You and New Hope's most easily remembered telephone number since 9-1-1?"

"Very funny. Just because she's always been popular is no reason to assume she was, or is, easy."

Spoken like a typical man whose brains had gone south. From the stories Jenny remembered, the leggy blonde—whose ambitions for fame and fortune had included campaigning for everything with a title attached to it, from Miss Register Your Pet onward—had developed quite a reputation almost from the minute she reached puberty. It came as no surprise when she left New Hope as soon as possible for points farther west, toward Hollywood to be exact.

"Where on earth did you run into her?" Jenny asked, not bothering to hide her distaste.

Mitch looked as if he would rather confess to making obscene phone calls than answer. "Our fifteen-year class reunion last fall."

"She came to *that?* What happened? Weren't they casting for any mouthwash or bug spray commercials that weekend?"

"Where's this venom coming from?" He flexed his shoulders and shoved his hands into his pockets, looking anything but comfortable. "At any rate, you were just a kid back when she and I were in high school. What were you, in the fifth— No, it was the sixth grade."

She was too angry and hurt to be impressed with his memory, but he was right. It had been the year her parents died while on one of her father's business trips. She'd been sent to live with her grandmother in this house, and promptly developed a lifelong crush on Mitch.

He had a point, though. She had no right to jump to quick conclusions about Savannah. She hadn't known her, except by reputation and to see her around town. Any negative reactions she had were strictly the result of the green-eyed monster taking control.

She looked down at the baby, grateful that she could see no resemblance to the woman whatsoever. It made it easier to apologize. "You're right, that was long ago."

"I'm not saying Savannah was perfect."

Good. That would save her from the temptation of throwing the baby bottle at him. "I shouldn't have been so quick to condemn her," she replied with a sweet smile. She could, however, just imagine what her grandmother would have to say about this. Her last surviving relative had always seen Mitch as a scoundrel in wolf's clothing.

The only two good things you can say for the man, Jenny, love, is that he doesn't pretend to be anything

*other than what he is, and that he looks mighty fine in
that uniform.*

No, her grandmother would not like hearing that it
was New Hope's most notorious vamp who'd joined
with the town wolf to make this lovely child. It would
mean yet another round of lectures about how Jenny
had wasted years spinning dreams about the man.

"I'm not denying that Savannah's a sensual-loving
woman," Mitch said, avoiding her gaze. "The thing
is . . . well, wherever she got that reputation . . . it wasn't
from me."

"But you always wanted her," Jenny added, although she hated having to admit knowing that.

"At seventeen or eighteen with my hormones rag-
ing? C'mon, Jen." He made a face. "And . . . I guess I
got a bit starstruck when she noticed me at the reunion."

Jenny supposed she could understand that, too. She'd
seen Savannah in a few commercials and had to admit
the woman was holding up well for someone approaching her mid-thirties. Though that didn't quite keep Jen
from wishing the woman stretch marks from her tummy
to her ears!

Her disgruntled thoughts yielded to one of curiosity.
"Was it worth it?"

Mitch considered the question for a moment, his gaze
ultimately shifting to the baby. "Under the circumstances, I don't think that's a fair question to ask."

Right again. Jenny decided she would do well to re-
direct their conversation away from Savannah for the
time being. "I take it you won't be flying today?"

"Of course not. Being a pilot for a national airline
isn't exactly like riding bumper cars at the amusement

park. If you don't make your flight, you don't just climb into the next one available and take off."

"But you called in to explain that an emergency forced you to ask for someone to take your place." He'd told her that much before. "Surely they understood?"

"Yeah, they understood. But they don't want their people to make a habit out of finding excuses not to fly."

"You mean, you're in trouble?"

"Not to the point where I have to worry about ferrying yak to Timbuktu in the foreseeable future. But I have to get my life in order, and fast. Seniority notwithstanding, in this age of corporate cutbacks, there's always another qualified pilot waiting to take your job."

The baby finished her bottle. Jenny set it on the table, then she shifted the child to an upright position against her shoulder.

"What are you doing now?"

"Helping her food settle in her tummy." Ever so lightly, Jenny patted the baby's back through the soft blankets she had come wrapped in. Within seconds a delicate burp erupted from the child. Jenny smiled at Mitch's startled expression. "See?"

"I'll be."

"Sometimes she'll spit up a bit, so you'll want to put a dishtowel or a napkin on your shoulder to protect your clothes."

"How did you know to do that?"

He sounded as if this was something you could only learn through membership in a secret society. "Quite a few of my friends have children, and it's not as if the subject of babies isn't on TV and everywhere else. Haven't you been paying attention to what's going on around you, McCord?"

He gave her a guilty look. "I guess not. Obviously I'm going to have to take a crash course, at least until I can get my hands on Savannah and find out what she was trying to prove by dumping— Er, by doing this." No sooner did he say that than he made a deep-throated sound and ran his hands through his hair. "What am I talking about? What difference does it make how fast I try to learn how to care for a baby? I have a job that takes me across the country and back four days a week. I can't take a kid with me on a 737!"

Jenny couldn't have asked for a better opening line. "Would you like me to watch her while you're gone? Until you decide what you're going to do, that is."

His expression was something between relief and incredulity. "Just like that? You want to help me? Even though you know whose child she probably is?"

"I'm glad you put it that way." Jenny was honest enough to admit she wanted something out of this for herself, even if it only turned out to be simply earning his respect. She resettled the baby in her arms and smiled down at the content child. "But the point is, none of this is this little darling's fault, and . . . I do like *one* of her parents."

"Damn, Jen, that's . . ." Mitch hunkered down in front of her and took her hand in his. "I can't tell you what your help will mean to me. And I'll pay you, of course."

She should have suffered whiplash for the speed with which she went from pleased to indignant. She snatched her hand back. "You'll do no such thing! For your information I love children, and having a tidbit like this one around will be no inconvenience at all."

"But, honey, you have a business of your own to worry about."

Jenny forced herself not to be swayed by the careless endearment, although deep inside her heart did handsprings. "Don't you worry about my business. In case you haven't noticed, women have been proving themselves capable of doing more than one thing at a time for centuries. All I ask is that you think twice about being so quick to locate Savannah. She's already proved what kind of mother material she is by today's actions. What if after you gave the baby back to her, she turned around and offered it up for adoption? *Your* daughter?"

To his credit, Mitch's whole body went stiff, his eyes flashed with 24-karat anger. "She damn well better not!" But he also looked less than ready to convict Savannah entirely. "Still, there is such a thing as mitigating circumstances."

Jenny could imagine what they might be. No doubt Savannah had seen a baby and motherhood as cramping her social life, something that made her seem older, less sensual than an ambitious actress might want to appear.

She shrugged. "Maybe. In any case, think about it. And while you're at it, don't you think you should tell me what I'm supposed to call this little angel?"

Chapter Two

Mitch didn't want to get testy, but between Brad and his cohorts at the police station and those viper-tongued mercenaries in white at the hospital, this was the tenth time he'd been asked about the baby's name, and he'd only *had* the kid for a couple hours! Jenny's query proved to be one too many.

"You tell me!" he snapped, throwing up his hands. "Haven't you heard anything I said? We haven't been formally introduced yet. I'm only *assuming* the kid is Savannah's. Until I get her to admit it— Ah, heck."

It came as no surprise that the baby began whimpering again. Reduced to feeling more of a heel than before, Mitch shut his eyes and shook his head. Until today he'd been known as a pretty levelheaded, calm guy. But thanks to this situation he was beginning to feel as if he was one step away from a straitjacket.

Jenny's look spoke volumes as she began rocking the baby and making soothing sounds. She reminded Mitch of his school days, when he would get reproving looks for talking in class or passing notes to his latest focus of interest.

"Sorry," he mumbled, just as he had at eight, twelve, fifteen, and so on. He added a crooked smile, hoping it worked as well as it used to.

After only seconds, Jenny relented. "You're under a great deal of pressure. I understand that. But you are going to have to watch the tone of your voice. This little one may not understand the words you say, but she can sense the angry tone."

"I'm not angry, I'm frustrated. And scared. But I know what you said makes sense." Everything made sense coming out of her mouth. It's when *he* spoke that things ceased to add up. "You're very good at this. At adapting."

"I have the easier role here. This isn't my shock to handle."

"Thanks for understanding that…that this is a shock to me." He wondered if she understood the depth of his gratitude and the concern his gratitude triggered.

"But you *are* going to have to think of a name for this baby."

Gently nudged out of his musing, he frowned. "Look, I told you…" He paused. Reconsidered. "Is that fair? I mean, she probably already has a name."

"One, at least. McCord."

Struck by the reality of the situation all over again, Mitch experienced a strange, almost surreal feeling. He stared down at the tiny bundle in Jenny's arms. To think he'd recently been accepting the possibility that he might never marry or have children. His own childhood hadn't been all that great, what with his parents divorcing when he was barely out of diapers, and then bouncing him from one home to another for years as they played out their animosities, using him as both weapon and trophy. He'd vowed that no kid of his was going to have to go through that. Yet here was blood of his blood—his daughter—and Savannah had already pulled a coup by dropping the child on his front steps!

Lost in thought, he wasn't aware of Jenny rising until she stood directly in front of him and eased the baby into his arms. "What . . . Oh, I don't think—"

"Take her. Be careful to support her head and neck, though. Her bones are incredibly fragile at this age."

So were his nerves. Mitch felt alarm bells going off throughout his body. The kid wasn't small, she was minute! He'd slept on pillows that weighed more. Holding her gave him the most panicky feeling, as if she might slip through his arms! Incredible.

"You feel as if you're embracing a miracle, don't you?"

"Something damned breakable, at any rate."

"You're a very lucky man, Mitch."

Despite the lump that threatened to form in his throat, he didn't quite know if he believed her. Granted, this was one cute kid, but the circumstances under which she'd come into his life simply underscored how little he deserved to be holding such a healthy and lovely child. Good grief, he and Savannah had been beyond careless, they'd been stupid.

"What do you think I should call her?" he murmured, lifting his bewildered and troubled gaze.

The smile that perennially hovered around Jenny's mouth blossomed into a full-fledged grin. "Whatever you like, I suppose. In a way, Savannah's forfeited her right to name her. What feels good to you? People often name a daughter after a mother or grandmother, or some relation they care deeply about.''

He thought of his family—or rather lack of one. That narrowed things down a great deal. So much so that he had nothing to offer.

After several seconds Jenny said, ''Your mother's alive, isn't she?''

Sometimes cockeyed optimists were more headache than antidote. ''Here's a news flash—I would name this baby Pepperoni before I named her after my mother.''

''Aha. Guess her d-i-v-o-r-c-e from your dad is still a touchy subject. Okay, then…surely there's some other name that's stood out in your mind as being special? Something traditional like Ann, or Kathy, or Mary? Names that are stronger like Taylor or Madison? How about—''

''Mary.''

''Exactly. Um, you like that?''

She sounded somewhat taken aback by his choice. ''What's wrong with it? You're the one who suggested something traditional first.''

''I know, but it's…maybe *too* old-fashioned? For you, I mean?''

Since when was he not supposed to like old-fashioned? The name had a comforting sweetness to it. Besides, he wanted his daughter to be called something that made her think twice about following in her parents' footsteps, about reacting in haste and succumbing to restlessness, about not thinking of consequences enough.

''I'll go with Mary,'' he said with new resolve. Mary…for as long as he had her.

Jenny stroked the blond peach fuzz at the top of the baby's head before putting her little finger into the child's tiny hand and shaking gently. "Hello, Mary McCord. How nice to meet you."

The infant responded with a fleeting smile.

Mitch sucked in a quick breath. "Did you see that?"

"I think you have a smart young lady there, Mc-Cord."

"Yeah." He rode a wave of pride high, and exhaled in pleasure.

"What do you say I give you a few pointers as I change her?"

"Change her?" The two words brought him back to earth with a resounding thump that left his insides quaking.

"This may be a news bulletin, my friend, but a sum of what goes into this cutie is going to come out the other end. In other words, I've a hunch that the milk I just fed her has had time to work. I'd rather walk you through the diaper-changing process now, so you don't call me at two in the morning in a panic."

"You're right, of course, but— Oh, man. Jenny, diapers?"

"You want to play, you gotta pay, Friendly Skies. Gran made a few diapers out of some old T-shirts we had, but I hope you picked up some disposables. Something tells me you won't be up to handling the washable kind."

She had that right. He had yet to deal with the idea that when he left here, he would be taking the baby with him. Having to take Jen's teasing on top of that was asking a bit much. "I hope you're enjoying yourself. To think all these years I believed you weren't capable of saying anything that wasn't kind or supportive." He thought that might earn him some expression of regret or chagrin.

She grinned irreverently. "Who did you think you had as a neighbor? The Flying Nun?"

Not quite. Maybe more like what's-her-name from *The Sound of Music*. But he supposed he had no right to expect her to be different than the others. This was, after all, nothing less than he deserved. On the other hand...

"Poor McCord. You look like a character in those old silent movies who finds himself racing down the street with a steering wheel loose in his hands."

"Actually, I feel worse."

Jenny nodded, studying him. "It's not your situation that brings out this side of me," she began more gently, "so much as the way you typecast me. You don't really know me, Mitch. You shouldn't assume that you do."

But the way he'd seen her had been safe, and he couldn't begin to explain that without dropping himself into a different stew altogether. Glum, he gazed down at the baby.

Jenny muttered something under her breath. "Oh, stop acting like an abused basset hound, and come with me. I'll show you what to do." Something new and flirtatious lit her eyes. "Maybe you'd better strip first, though."

"Ex*cuse* me?"

"Lose the jacket and tie." She took the baby from him. "And roll up your sleeves. As I told you before, working with babies can be rough on your wardrobe."

As annoyed at her spunkiness as he was wary about what lay ahead, Mitch did as directed, set the two items over the back of a dinette chair, then followed Jenny. They went in the opposite direction Fiona had gone, but the sound of the old woman grinding away at her knit-

ting machine while the TV blared was loud enough to
muffle their steps.

Jenny led him around the stairway and down the hall.
Mitch noted old family photographs placed in group-
ings on the wall like stepping stones along a garden
path. Most captured moments in various stages of Jenny's childhood: costumed as a teddy bear for her first
Halloween, her first day of school, her first visit with
Santa, the budding entrepreneur's first lemonade stand,
her first two-wheeler, her senior prom—he never did get
a glimpse of the guy who took her. She didn't give him
time to linger, which he decided was just as well. Who
needed reminders that Jenny had been a delightful and
charming child?

Once in the dusty-pink-tiled bathroom, Jenny set the
baby on a thick towel folded on the vanity. The setup
told Mitch that she'd already changed the child at least
once during his absence. A small stack of makeshift diapers was piled neatly by a bottle of baby lotion and
powder. Mitch eyed the plastic containers as Jenny ran
water into the sink, and deduced that she must use the
stuff herself. That would explain her wonderful skin,
and why she always smelled uniquely fresh and young.
It also reminded him of why it was wise to keep as much
distance as possible between them.

Seduced by baby products... ridiculous.

Only when she shut off the water and dipped her elbow into the bowl, did he snap out of his brooding. He
frowned. "What are you doing?"

"Checking the temperature. What feels acceptable to
our fingers could well burn her tender skin. The wrist
and elbow are usually more sensitive. You try it."

Pushing up his sleeve a bit more, Mitch did. "Feels
tepid to me."

"That'll be more than enough for her. Now, go ahead and unwrap her."

He froze. "I'd prefer to watch . . . at least once."

"You know that you learn faster by doing. And you know full well that I'm not going to let you do something that could hurt the child."

She proved as good as her word. For the next several minutes she corrected him a number of times as she supervised and assisted him. Once again Mitch thought that for someone without children of her own, she was impressively competent. And she was able to be kind when criticizing. That had him sending up another prayer of gratitude that she wasn't more like her grandmother.

He could have done with less physical contact, though. Time after time their hands brushed together, or she wove an arm between or around his to show him how to balance the child in the crook of his arm during bathing, how to apply the lotion and powder, where the pins needed to go. He could have lived a full life without being reminded that Jenny's skin could compete with the newborn's for softness, or experiencing her breast pressed intimately against his upper arm, or discovering that her body fit ever so nicely against his. By the time they were refastening the baby's sleeper, Mitch's mouth felt as dry as if he'd just come through a West Texas dust storm.

"Good for you," Jenny said, ever the good cheerleader. "In a few more days you'll be able to do this in the pitch dark if you have to."

"I'd rather not. As it is, I can't imagine doing this a couple dozen times a day," he muttered, using his sleeve to wipe at his sweaty forehead. "I feel as if I've run the Boston and New York marathons back-to-back."

A soft laugh bubbled from Jenny's lips. "Don't exaggerate. You're going to be wonderful with her."

"Now who's exaggerating?" Clipped at the knees by his strong awareness of her, Mitch let his gaze roam over her glossy hair, her radiant profile. He didn't know whether it was his gruff tone, or his obvious gratitude, but in the next second she shifted and he found himself made more vulnerable by looking straight into her eyes. Inches apart, he would only have to duck his head to discover at last if her dewy lips would feel half as good as they looked and taste as sweet as the stuff she concocted in her kitchen.

It was Jenny who turned away. With deft movements she quickly finished wrapping the baby in the blanket. "Between the two of us, I'm sure we can keep Mary comfortable. What do you say, sweetie?" she asked the baby as she lifted it into her arms again.

Mitch stood alone in the bathroom before he realized just how smoothly he'd been manipulated. Like a minnow being toyed with by a wily bass, she'd drawn him in and spit him out. As intrigued as he was annoyed, he hurried to catch up with her.

"What do you mean, the two of us? I'm the one who has to figure out how to deal with her through tonight. That is, unless you could come next door with me and help me get her settled?"

"An invitation to The Bachelor Pad? Be still my heart."

He supposed he deserved that, since he'd never before let her beyond the screen door. What she couldn't know was that his motive had always been based on self-preservation.

"If you're expecting to see satin sheets and handcuffs, you're going to be disappointed."

Her answering look was the picture of innocence. "I doubt you'd need the toys and hardware."

Following that with a comment about wanting to inform her grandmother where she would be, Jenny left him for a moment. Mitch used the brief respite to justify what he was doing; Jenny had a tendency to make him forget. After years of dealing with her wistful looks and hopeful invitations, her behavior a few moments ago had come as quite a surprise. Her actions had clearly signaled no. But what had he seen in her eyes? What was going on?

Jenny returned and they exited her house. Once outside Mitch noticed how much the weather had deteriorated. The sky had grown much darker, and the wind had picked up to the point that Jenny had to fold one corner of the blanket over the baby's face to protect her. After unlocking the side door on his brick home to let Jenny get the baby to safety, Mitch hurried to his car to collect the things he'd picked up from the hospital and during his brief stop at the Baby Boutique.

"We have a crib up in the attic that you're welcome to use," Jenny told him as he joined her inside and set the boxes and bags on the kitchen table.

"Thanks, but don't forget, I'm not sure I'll have the baby long enough to trouble with all that."

Her expression fell. "I thought— Didn't you say you didn't approve of what Savannah had done?"

"If she *is* the mother. Remember, I also said I don't have proof. Until I find Savannah and she admits to this, any long-term decisions about the baby, and settling her in here, should be put on hold."

Jenny's expression told him what she thought of his hedging again. "And how are you going to get Savannah to do that? Do you have any idea where she is?"

"No. But Brad referred me to a detective he's worked with before. Says the guy's reliable. I'll try making a few phone calls myself, and if they don't pan out, I'll give him a call."

"It would seem to me that if she went to this much trouble to leave Mary without talking to you, she won't be taking any calls from you, either."

That had crossed his mind, too. "I still have to make the gesture."

"Too bad it's at the expense of your daughter."

Mitch stiffened. "I appreciate the help, Jen, but don't push too hard, okay?"

"One comes with the other, McCord." But having said her piece, she quickly fixed a pleasant smile on her face and glanced around. "So this is how it looks in here."

He eyed the kitchen that was a cool two-tone blue, as opposed to the sunny yellow, white and green of Jenny's place. It also stood out for its lack of cooking accoutrements; and since he rarely prepared his own meals, it lacked the delicious smells that had emanated from the Stevenses' stove.

"Home sweet home," he drawled as a deep roll of thunder rumbled something in the house.

"Going to give me a tour?"

"It's just a house, Jen. Four walls and a decent tax write-off."

"It's your *home*. Your daughter is going to sleep here. If it's too grim, too drafty, too stuffy, someone has to point that out to you."

But he wasn't wild about her wandering around the place, analyzing and judging, not to mention touching, so that no matter where he stepped or sat in the future, mental images of her would flash before his eyes. "I'd rather be going for root canal work than doing this," he mumbled, running a hand over his hair.

"Pardon?"

"I said I'm not the most consistent housekeeper. You don't know what you might be in for."

"Nonsense. So far everything looks fine to me."

She kissed the baby on the forehead, and ventured toward the living room, also dark, despite the white walls. It was decorated in greens and browns with old but solid furniture, most of which hadn't been replaced or moved since Mitch's father bought the house. The center of focus was the big-screen TV and extensive video and CD collection.

"I have a feeling the only thing I'll end up mentioning is that this place is too shut up," she told him.

She slowed to browse through the built-in bookshelves where the tapes and CDs were stacked. Mitch couldn't remember the last time he'd dusted them.

"This is a surprise."

He edged closer. "What is?"

"Your video collection could be mine—a heavy dose of comedy, but some serious drama, too."

"I have fairly diverse taste, but prefer a story to have some meat to it."

"Me, too. Gran's the one who likes the action and shoot-'em-up films."

"I know. In cooler weather when she works with the windows open, she plays her TV so loud I could swear there's a police raid going on at your place. She can make sleeping late on a Saturday or Sunday quite a challenge."

"That's why I wear my earphones so much when I'm working," Jenny replied with a sympathetic look over her shoulder. "But don't worry, she'll behave with the baby in the house."

After flipping through several more videos, she focused on the CDs—and made a surprised sound. "Who would have thought it?"

Now what?

"Soft rock...the classics...the Blues...and New Age!"

Mitch didn't have to guess what she was driving at. "New Age...what a term for art and philosophy that's really centuries old."

"I couldn't agree more."

"In any case, it's soothing after a stressful day."

"True. I like to listen when I'm having a long, luxurious bubble bath."

Help. It was too easy to picture Jenny with her hair piled high, her luscious skin dewy.... Fortunately, a particularly loud crack of thunder sounded and Mitch's attention was drawn to the baby, who'd started at the sharp sound.

"Maybe we'd better finish the tour," he told Jenny. "Before the electricity goes and we can't see too well."

Like hers, his house had two floors, but with fewer nooks and crannies. He'd also turned the sun-drenched recreation room into his private gym.

"So this is how you keep in shape," Jenny said.

"Well, flying's not the most physical of occupations. If I didn't do something, I'd be a wreck."

"You used to run. Why did you stop?"

"Running *and* playing tennis proved tough on my knees. I decided I didn't want to give up tennis, so I opted for weights and machines instead."

"Oh—and you have a green thumb!" Jenny cried, doing a full three-sixty to eye the lush plants lining the length of the floor-to-ceiling windows.

"Hardly. I asked around for something easy to grow, had a nursery write down simple directions, and basically ignored the plants otherwise." Not wanting her to see how much her admiration meant to him, Mitch encouraged her to move on. "C'mon. You might as well see the rest of the place."

He gestured toward the stairs and let her go first so he could catch her if she stumbled. Following allowed him to watch her careful and protective treatment of the baby, the sway of her slim hips under the maroon-and-rose print of her jumper, and her slender ankles beneath her annoyingly long skirt. The sigh he indulged in at the top betrayed an inner conflict growing faster than he could have expected.

His house was slightly larger than the Stevenses' place and consisted of four upstairs bedrooms to their three. After one huge walk-in storage closet, they passed the room that had been his as a boy, then another, the main bathroom, and finally they came to the two bedrooms at the far end of the house.

"The baby will probably do well here," Jenny told him, indicating the room across from the master bedroom.

Mitch frowned. "What's wrong with my old one? Or the guest room?"

"They're too far away."

"A few yards isn't that much."

"It makes all the difference. If you're in a deep sleep, you'll never hear her if she cries."

"But I use that room for an office," he said, gesturing to the third bedroom.

"So move the desk, file cabinets and whatnot down to the other room. How much trouble can that be for a strong man like you?"

Flattery would get her nowhere. "You're determined to make sure I never get a minute of sleep again, aren't you?"

"That's not the issue. All right, how about setting her crib in your room for now?"

"Oh, no."

"People do that all the time."

But did they sleep in the nude the way he did? Mitch knew he wasn't about to ask her that. "I don't think that's a habit I want to start."

"Then I definitely suggest the room across from yours."

"I'll think about it," he said, hedging to buy time.

Giving him a look that told him she neither understood nor approved of his stubbornness, she crossed into his room. It was what he'd been dreading most. At least he hadn't overslept and had taken the time to make the bed.

Like the other rooms, the walls were a textured white, the carpet a thick, champagne pile, and the furnishings designed in clean, sturdy lines to accommodate his size. Boring. But as Jenny stood in front of the king-size bed, her back to him, thoughts of design slipped from his mind, and all he could imagine was a scenario where he stretched her across the blue-and-green spread and lowered himself over her. She would look like a mermaid with her hair fanning across the deep-sea-colored covering.

"It's different than I expected."

His fantasy vanished like a popped soap bubble. "I told you that I lean toward the uncomplicated, easy-to-maintain look."

"I didn't mean I don't like it. It's nice. Very clean. That's important for the baby."

Mitch grimaced. Boy was she ever reaching for something pleasant to say. On the other hand, what had he expected? Sure, he'd lived here for the better part of his life, when he hadn't been dragged over half of Europe by his mother and her latest spouse, but he'd collected no souvenirs of happy trips, no treasured gifts from a parent. Even his sports trophies from his school days were shoved back deep into bookcases where they could serve some purpose as bookends.

The only adornments in the room were an onyx-and-brass alarm clock on the bed stand he had bought himself, along with the two brass-and-wood lamps with deep blue shades, and the leather case on the dresser, which held his watch, college ring, a few pairs of cuff links and some tie tacks. He received his pleasure from *doing* not *collecting*.

"At least you don't have to deal with the hot afternoon sun."

While he'd been brooding, Jenny had moved on to peer out one of the bedroom windows. He knew she was noting the position of his room to hers. They were directly across from each other, a point that sometimes tempted Mitch to move back into his old room, except that he liked the master bath that came with this one.

He cleared his throat. "It would be cooler if you lowered your blinds." Especially when she was sleeping.

"I know, but I like watching the moon and stars before I fall asleep."

She *liked* driving him crazy with views of her prancing around in her lacy poet shirts and other equally feminine nighties before climbing into bed. Mitch rubbed the back of his neck. The rain started to beat a strong tattoo on the window. It was his favorite weather for curling up for a lazy afternoon.

"I thought you were going to help me get the baby settled?" he asked, almost sounding desperate.

"Sure, but you still haven't decided in which room you're going to let her stay. For the time being, though, this will do, won't it, Mary?" she said, placing the baby in the middle of the bed.

To Mitch's dismay, she half sat, half lay down beside the child and began using the pillows to build a frame around the infant. What a picture...Jenny, looking like a flower, her cheeks no less pink than her T-shirt, her thick dark braid caressing her breast with every move. Small wonder his child was already gazing up at her with wonder. Before long she would have Mary not only doting but relying on her.

If he wasn't careful, he would end up needing Jenny too much himself. It was a terrifying thought, considering the track record he came from.

"There." Giving Mary a tender kiss on her forehead, Jenny rose from the bed and crossed to Mitch. "All right."

He lifted an eyebrow as she reached up, took the jacket and tie that he'd slung over his shoulder, and tossed them on the armchair behind him. "All right?" he asked.

"Now she can sleep and *we* can get to it."

Chapter Three

Get to it... get to it... get to it.

Jenny's provocative statement haunted Mitch all night. He should have known it had been harmless on her part—merely her way to initiate going through the baby's things and setting up a work space and routine for caring for Mary. But between what his imagination had concocted, and his later concern that the child was safe in her basket bed, well, he'd done well to get any sleep.

By four o'clock the next morning, he gave up, and by five, Mitch had showered, dressed in his uniform, changed and fed the baby, and *changed her again.* Now he was peeking out between the slats of his bedroom blinds to make sure Jenny was awake.

It was time to take Mary next door. If he didn't leave by six, he could easily get tied up in traffic. Missing yet another flight just wasn't going to happen. But going next door and facing Jenny again, after what he'd endured yesterday, was asking a great deal.

"Come on, McCord. All you have to do is get in and get out."

That's the way he should do it. No lingering, not too much small talk. He could manage. With any luck, she would be so eager to get her hands on the baby, she would hardly be aware that he'd escaped.

The lights were bright in the kitchen and dinette windows, and he could see Jenny bustling around, preparing to get the bulk of her cooking and baking done before the heat of the day set in. She had managed to eke out a seemingly decent living for herself with her little specialty business, as had her grandmother by creating designer-quality knit apparel. That was virtually all Mitch knew about what they did, and all he wanted to know.

He went to collect the baby. Mary had fallen asleep again and now barely stirred as he carried her downstairs, then from his house to the Stevenses'. Yesterday's downpour had cleansed the air, allowing the heady fragrances from Jenny's flower beds to flirt with his senses as Mitch climbed the stairs that led to her kitchen. Fully expecting to knock, Jenny surprised him by opening the door before he reached the landing.

"Good morning! Come in, come in."

"She's sleeping," Mitch whispered back at her.

Jenny nodded and held the door open for him. "How'd it go last night? You were on my mind."

No wonder he hadn't gotten any sleep. With all the mental energy going on between their houses, it was a wonder they hadn't set off every electrical appliance in the area. But Mitch hid his thoughts with a benign smile. "Fine."

"Really? Your eyes are bloodshot."

"They always are at this hour."

The white eyelet shirt and peasant skirt Jenny wore under an old-fashioned frilly apron gave her the kind of feminine, romantic appeal an Impressionist painter would find irresistible to recapture. Mitch all but scraped the back of his jacket against the opposite doorjamb to avoid physical contact with her, afraid of what the slightest touch might do to his resistance.

"You should try cucumber slices...or better yet, cooled tea bags. With the excess moisture squeezed out, of course."

Because of his own cerebral gymnastics, she'd lost him. "Squeeze tea bags—for what?"

"Relief. Your eyes. The tea leaves will reduce swelling, too." Jenny tilted her head for a better view of the baby. "She's precious. Did she keep you up all night?"

"Not at all." That was something he wanted to take up with Jenny. "She didn't even rouse for her 2:00 a.m. feeding as you warned she would."

Jenny chuckled. "So why are you complaining? I said she *might* wake up. Maybe you're lucky to have one of the perfect models."

But Mitch could tell she was surprised and...a bit miffed that he'd lucked out in getting a kid that well behaved.

"Where should I put her?" he asked. "She shouldn't be exposed to too much noise." He didn't care if that made him sound like a know-it-all. But to his relief, Jenny took it—him—in stride.

"The living room for now. Later after Gran gets up and turns on the TV, I'll figure out someplace better. Here, let me have that tote first."

Once Faith Harper at the Baby Boutique heard Mitch was going to ask Jenny to baby-sit while he was gone, she had talked him into buying a quilted shoulder bag for the baby's paraphernalia. On his way home yesterday he'd worried that Faith would phone Jen before he had a chance to present his case. No telling what he would be doing now if things hadn't worked out.

While Jenny set the bag on a kitchen chair, he put the baby on the couch in the living room, lingering to watch her. A strange contraction gripped his heart. A silly feeling, when he thought about it. They'd only been together a few hours, hardly long enough to feel any real attachment. But looking at her sweet, peaceful expression and noting how her little bow mouth puckered and worked, he knew that if there was any way around it, he would have happily phoned in and asked for someone to relieve him on today's flight, as well.

With a sigh he backed away and returned to the kitchen.

"Time for a cup of coffee?" Jenny asked, her big brown eyes romance-novel limpid as she gazed up at him.

"Better not. I need to try to make up some points from yesterday." He dug into his pocket and pulled out a note he'd written earlier. "Here's a few phone numbers in case something—"

"Everything will be fine, Mitch."

"Yeah, but you should be able to reach me no matter what. I'll leave a message at the airport to let them know that if you call you should be put through right away."

"Thanks," she said softly. "I do appreciate you making yourself so accessible."

Too accessible. Now there wouldn't be a corner available for him to hide in where Jenny couldn't find him if she chose to initiate a hunt. There would be no escape from her melodious voice, no avoiding thoughts of her, no forgetting that he would have to deal with her all over again when he got back.

He gestured toward the tote. "Anyway, I put a little of everything I had in there. If it's not enough..." He began to reach for his wallet.

Jenny grabbed his arm. "Don't you dare start that. I know your IOU is as good as gold."

He meant to remove her hand, but somehow his hand had developed a mind of its own. Suddenly he found himself closing his fingers around hers. He looked down to see how much larger and tanned he was in comparison, and despite her hard work, how much softer her skin felt. It brought back a familiar curiosity and temptation that always taunted him when he found himself in her presence.

Swallowing, he met her watchful gaze. "I can't tell you how much I appreciate this, Jen."

"I know you do. It's written all over your face."

What else did she see there? His troubled feelings and attraction for her? God help him, he hoped not. Jenny was a decent girl. *Woman*. She deserved better than an emotional coward like him.

Something of his feelings must have telegraphed itself to her, because before he could back away, she reached up and kissed his cheek.

"Don't worry, McCord. Your little girl is in the best hands." The next thing he knew, she was pushing him toward the door. "Now get out of here before you end up missing another flight and deprive me of getting to play with your daughter."

"I do still need to get my bag and lock up the house," he said, mostly to regain his psychological footing.

"If you want to call when you arrive at LAX, feel free."

"Sounds good. I'll probably do that."

"Have a safe flight."

She seduced him with attentiveness: a sweep across his shoulder to brush away a piece of lint, a quick tug to bring him closer and adjust his collar, a tender rub of his back to bolster him emotionally. It was all Mitch could do not to peck her on the lips as he headed out the door. But he was no Ward Cleaver. If he got that close to Jenny Stevens's delectable mouth, he would be darned if he would settle for some chaste insect bite of a kiss!

"Yeah," he murmured seconds after she shut the door behind him. He glanced over his shoulder to stare at the thick, weather-darkened screen and heavier wood barrier between them. "'Bye."

Jenny pressed her ear to the door to listen to Mitch leave, a foolish grin curving her lips. Preoccupied, she almost missed the shuffling sound behind her.

"And exactly what do you think you're up to?"

She should have known the Human Radar would show up. With an inner sigh, she faced her grandmother. "Morning! You're up earlier than usual. I'll get your coffee."

"Not so fast. I saw that little smile on your face and it's not reassuring."

"Since when is it a crime to be pleasant and strive for a positive attitude? Aren't you always muttering about how you hate your habit of scowling and how it puckers this and wrinkles that? Now I'm trying to avoid the same thing and you're picking on me.''

Not a muscle moved on her grandmother's round, apple-cheeked face. ''You have your grandfather's quick mind and fast tongue.''

''Not just his. I have some of your genes, too.'' Unafraid of what her grandmother would throw at her, because as nagging as the woman could get, she was still a dear and had only Jen's best interests in mind, Jenny headed for the coffee machine. ''And what's wrong with being pleased at how things are working out?''

''You call this working out? Mr. Friendly Skies got himself into a mess and he turned to you because you're convenient. But you, with that stardust in your eyes, you see nothing ahead of you but fair flying weather and a bridal bouquet.''

''Don't get overly dramatic.''

Fiona uttered a soft snort as she accepted the mug of steaming coffee and added milk from the creamer Jenny had already set out. ''I don't know where I went wrong.''

''That's because you didn't.''

''I raised you as carefully as I could. Instilled in you a respect for people, a pride in food and home. Why, you've made a name for yourself as someone who cares about what you produce. You have the most charming, responsible bachelors in New Hope knocking at your door—''

''A result of you hustling dates for me at church and the market.''

''Hustling? What kind of word is that to use in this house?''

''You hustle, dear heart.''

Her grandmother averted her gaze and patted her sleep-flattened hair. "I'm your grandmother. It's my privilege. And does any of this make an impression on you? No. You only have eyes for a man who'll never settle down because he's been flying at such high altitude for so long it's affected his brain."

"Gran!"

"Well, what other explanation is there for a man who doesn't react the way decent, *normal* people do?"

Jenny rolled her eyes, as much in frustration as for knowing peace and quiet wasn't this easy to come by. "You should have gone on stage, Gran. Or into politics. Your ability to take your color-crayon theories and turn them into logic is truly remarkable."

As if she hadn't spoken, her grandmother took a calm, careful sip of coffee. She looked like an Oriental matriarch in the emerald green robe Jenny had given her last Christmas. But Jenny knew better than to assume this little skirmish was over.

"Make your jokes," Fiona intoned, her dark eyes still penetrating at seventy-five. "I'm only an old woman. Who cares what I think or feel? Soon I'll be with your grandfather, may he rest in peace, and then there'll be no one to save you against making the mistake of your life."

"He's attracted to me, Gran."

"Who wouldn't be? You're lovely, sweet, hardworking—"

"You forgot house-trained."

Her grandmother narrowed her eyes. "But such a mouth."

"That I definitely got from *you*."

"Nevertheless, I will bet you—"

"Not Julio again."

"Value is value. You just don't appreciate good music. What I'm trying to say is that your Captain Mc-Cord is probably attracted to a different woman every day. Maybe he can't help himself—look at his mother. The point is, he's not right for you. Do yourself a favor. Don't open yourself to heartbreak."

"I haven't and I'm not," she said, not entirely truthful. "Have you seen me chasing him?"

"Every chance you had since you were thirteen."

"I was a child with a crush. I mean, since I've grown."

"Correct me if I'm wrong, but wasn't it you who invited him for dinner last Christmas?"

"That doesn't count. That was the holidays. He lives alone and we had plenty. We would have been like Scrooges if we didn't ask him to join our party."

"Trying to talk sense to you makes my jaw ache."

A sure sign that her grandmother was yielding—at least a smidgen. Jenny put an arm around the smaller woman's shoulders. "Then put yourself out of misery and let's go peek at the baby."

So it went with all of their arguments, not that Jenny could really call them that. "Little fussings" is what she preferred to label them. It hadn't taken her long after she moved in to figure out that she was cut from the same cloth as her grandmother, and would have a sturdy streak of strength and opinion in her, no matter how hard she tried to soften it. She'd concluded that they could either spend the rest of their lives fighting like the blue jays that summered in the backyard, or she could learn to use that gift of humor and brains to work around the obvious pitfalls that awaited them.

Today they shared a bond deeper and more unbreakable than ever, and a love and respect that could get them through any skirmish. Even this one, which had been going on for years.

"Isn't she darling?" Jenny whispered as they bent over the basket.

"Of course. Absolutely. What we're arguing about is that she's another woman's baby, my dove."

The words came gently, allowing Jenny to nod and continue with equal care. "A woman who's proved she is and would be a terrible mother. Mary deserves better. If fate is at least a little fair, I'll see that she gets it."

Her grandmother looked from the baby to Jenny for several seconds, as if weighing the words before coming to her own conclusion. "Sometimes fairness alone isn't enough. Sometimes things aren't meant to be, no matter how hard we try to prove otherwise."

"This isn't one of those times."

"You do court your share of heartbreak, child."

Maybe, Jenny thought as she felt her grandmother slip an arm around her waist. But she had a feeling that when you were reaching for the best dreams, that was a fair price to pay.

"Good flight, Mitch," Neil Dennison said as the 737 came to a final stop at its designated LAX gate. The copilot unfastened his seat belt and reached for his clipboard to make some final notations. "You sure you don't want to join me for a bite to eat before we head back to Dallas? You look as if you could use something."

Something, but not food, Mitch thought with a slight grimace. "Thanks, but I'll have to pass. I have some calls I need to make."

"Problems?"

Neil had been flying with Mitch for six months now, and they'd known each other for almost three years. It came as no surprise to Mitch that Neil had been sensitive to his mood, and it allowed him to answer honestly. "You could say that."

"Does it have to do with why you had to take off yesterday?"

"And how." He met his sometime tennis partner's concerned gaze. "I found out I may be a father."

The dark-haired man lifted his eyebrows and whistled. "Whoa. That would get anyone's attention. How'd you find out?"

"By discovering a baby on my doorstep."

He quickly filled his friend in on the story. It felt good to talk to another guy about it, even though it was almost as embarrassing as when he'd told Jenny. But Neil was a decent guy beneath his good looks and, although Mitch knew there'd be some teasing down the road, his first and foremost reaction was concern.

"Son of a gun," he said. "How do you feel about that?"

"Stunned...confused...terrified."

Neil grinned. "You'd be that, regardless of whether you were anticipating her or not. Take it from someone who knows. The question is, do you think you'll be able to locate Savannah to make sure of all this?"

"I don't know. When she left town the next morning, she didn't give me a phone number or forwarding address, and to be honest, I didn't ask for one. But she is something of a celebrity. Surely she shouldn't be too difficult to find."

"You'd think." Inevitably, however, Neil's expression turned sly. "Well, I always thought you'd be caught sooner or later, but never quite like this."

"Hey, I'm nowhere near caught. Even if I find Savannah and prove paternity, I have no intention of marrying her. All that's important to me is making sure Mary has a good family and gets proper care."

"Will you keep her?"

There was that all-important question again. "To be honest, I don't know. What qualifications do I have to raise a kid, Neil? They need things like shots, feeding, attention."

"Are we discussing puppies or kids?"

"Interaction, is that better? A parent has to be there for a kid. Attend PTA, take field trips, spend the weekends at soccer fields and softball fields. My life is full as it is without all that."

"Only because you make it so."

How typical of Neil, since he had a two-year-old son of his own. "I could end up doing more damage than good."

"On the other hand, I doubt we'd ever have to worry about you leaving your kid on someone's doorstep, let alone walking away from her."

He had that right. Mitch didn't know if he could get over Savannah's actions. It was what made him committed to finding her, regardless of the cost. "No," he replied. "I wouldn't. That's why I have to use this time to check out some things."

"So do it. But don't discount your value in the process of child rearing. You matter more than you can imagine."

After thanking Neil for his best wishes, Mitch found a quiet spot to make some calls. On the top of his list was Jenny. He wanted to reassure himself that she was coping well with the baby.

At first he got her answering machine. "Jen? It's me. Are you there?"

There was a clicking, muffled sound before he heard her burst out with, "Hi! What's up?"

He liked her breathless voice and the energy behind it. "I'm in Los Angeles and wanted to check in."

"That's sweet. But your timing isn't. I'm neck-deep here. No time to talk."

She couldn't mean that, not after what she'd said before. "Do you mind if I ask how my daughter's doing?"

"Who?"

"Jen."

"Oh—*your* daughter. I didn't know if I heard right. Well, she's perfect. Better than. Why shouldn't she be?"

"I didn't mean to suggest—"

"Listen, if I don't get off this phone, I'm going to have twenty-five pounds of pear chutney to lug out and bury in the backyard, and that's not going to sit well with the restaurant down in Houston that's waiting for it."

Mitch's imagination worked overtime envisioning her wrestling with something out of a body snatchers movie. "Ah . . . sure. I didn't know you were— Jen, you're the one who said to call."

"Absolutely. Except for this critical moment. 'Bye!"

For several seconds Mitch stood there with the dead phone against his ear. Who did she think she was? He'd entrusted his child to her and the woman treated him as if he was a nuisance, shut him down, for pity's sake! He understood that she was busy, but she had to understand *his* need to reassure himself that Mary was all right.

Wait until he got home. As much as he appreciated what Jenny was doing for him, her sacrifice of time and effort, he wasn't about to let anyone treat him as if he were an annoying gnat.

Grim and determined, he dialed and reached for his telephone credit card once again. "Operator, I need information..."

It was the better part of forty minutes later when he checked his watch and decided he'd better start back to the plane. The phone calls he made after the one to Jenny hadn't proved much more successful than the first. In fact, the only positive result was that the detective Brad had referred him to was willing to come by the house this evening to discuss the matter of finding Savannah. He'd made *that* call after determining it would be impossible to locate her on his own—his several chats with various Information operators had proved that much. And it was clear after his conversation with Brad that his friend had no new information to share. The chief of police had only wanted to tease Mitch further about the unnerving situation.

Wholly preoccupied, Mitch didn't see the young woman who darted into his path. He barreled into her and had to grab her by her upper arms to keep her from falling backward into her two-wheeled carrier and bag. "Stacie?"

"Mitch!"

He steadied the pretty woman in the red, white and blue uniform, while he took in the Cleopatra hairdo and seductive smile framed in poppy-red lipstick. "I thought you had the New York to Greece run these days?" he asked.

"I do. I took a few days off to visit family out here. Long time no see. You look wonderful as ever."

"So do you." They exchanged hugs and Mitch's thoughts flashed back to the days when he and Stacie had been quite an item. It felt like a particularly long time ago.

"I was just on my way to grab a bite of lunch. Can you join me?"

The invitation should have tempted him. When Stacie took the New York to Athens run, she'd done it after a confrontation with him. She had wanted something beyond what they had. He had wanted to keep things as they were. Seeing her again should have had him wondering if he'd done the wrong thing in letting her go. To his surprise, he felt ... affection. Nothing more.

"I—I wish I could, Stace. But I'm due to head back to Dallas within the hour."

Her expression turned wry. "Story of my life where you're concerned. What's new in yours? Still playing the field?"

If she only knew. But he wasn't about to invite trouble. "In a different way now than then, because I don't want to hurt anyone. And I never wanted to hurt *you*, Stacie."

"I know that. Now." The smile she gave him said that she had survived and recovered, even if he did represent a temptation to her. "Seeing anyone in particular that I would know?"

"Ah ... no. I'm tied up with some, er, business these days. Too busy to really date much. You?"

"The same. I'm helping my kid sister open a café out here, and that's been keeping me preoccupied." But his news seemed to brighten her somewhat. She gave him another hug. "Well, if you ever change your mind, you know where to find me."

"You bet. Good seeing you again, Stace."

He stood there several seconds before she was swallowed up in the crowd coming off the 747 from Tokyo. *You have to be nuts.* What guy lets someone as sexy and *decent* as her slip through his fingers? Stacie hadn't asked for a wedding ring; all she'd wanted was someone to come home to on a steady basis, an agreement that they wouldn't date anyone else while they were together.

But he hadn't wanted anything to do with commitments.

With a shake of his head, Mitch continued walking toward his gate. He wondered if he would ever change his mind. His parents' lousy marriage sure had done a job on him. It was something he had to think about if it turned out that he and Mary were to be a family. The child would need full-time care when he wasn't around. He'd drafted Jenny because she'd been close, and . . . well, she just *looked* like she would be good with kids.

However, still smarting from the brush-off she'd delivered, he had to wonder if he'd been wrong to put so much confidence in her. Wasn't she proving that she was too busy with her own life to deal with a baby? It had only taken him one night with the little thing and he already had a good idea as to what such care entailed.

"You look worse now than you did before."

Mitch glanced over to see that Neil had fallen into step beside him. "I'm okay." For a guy hanging by his thumbs, he silently added with a twist of his lips.

"No luck with your detective work?"

"Nil. If Savannah is living in the Los Angeles area, her number's unlisted. Knowing her, though, she's probably shacked up with someone else. The Lone Ranger role never appealed to her." No, Savannah would hook up with someone who had the where-withal to keep her in style.

"So what's next, Captain Daddy?"

Mitch winced at the title. "Thanks, Dennison. You really know how to—"

"Captain *what?* Did I hear the word Daddy attrib-uted to you, Captain McCord, sir?"

With a groan, Mitch glanced over his shoulder to discover their senior flight attendant had fallen in be-hind them. "Lorna, I will pay for you and your hus-band to have dinner at the restaurant of your choice if you forget you heard that."

The redhead's laugh reminded him of Jenny's. Soft and musical, it wasn't mean, but it literally oozed mis-chief. "Tempting, but no deal. Confess or I'll grab that desk mike at the ticket counter and make a public an-nouncement."

She would, too. As with Neil, he'd known Lorna for several years and they'd flown many a mile together. He groaned up at the ceiling. "*Yes.* Okay? Feel better now?"

"You're looking at a man in deep pain, not to men-tion emotional turmoil," Neil told her with a wink. "I think he wants to ask us to be gentle with him."

"He wouldn't." The redhead's blue eyes twinkled with delight. "Oh, the things you hear when the mighty fall. So tell me, Captain, is the delightful event already here or coming?"

"She's here," Mitch said, feeling his shirt begin to stick to his back. "Her name is Mary, and she's beautiful, and innocent, and she doesn't deserve to become the center of ridicule, even if I do."

That earned him a look of surprise from Lorna that quickly turned to approval. "Good Lord...you almost sound like a father, Mitch. Do I know the mother?"

"No. She's someone from my past."

"What happens now?"

"I don't know."

"He only found out yesterday," Neil interjected in a conspiratorial whisper.

Lorna nodded. "No wonder you look as if you'd swallowed some bad oysters. Well, all I can say is that this is going to be the biggest news since Tawny Marshall quit Gulf-Pacific to marry that sheikh." She patted Mitch's back. "I'll tone down my teasing, but I hope you're not expecting miracles from everyone. You're just too inviting a target."

Didn't he know it. By the time they landed in Dallas Mitch felt as if he was wearing a bull's-eye on the back of his uniform.

He drove home feeling more drained than he had the first time he'd had his hands on the controls of a jumbo jet. Taking the back roads to avoid the jam on 635 didn't help, nor did listening to the radio. He knew that more stress lay ahead of him. And that even if he survived that, tomorrow he would have to do it all over again. The idea wasn't appealing. But it was nothing compared to the thought of being responsible for another human life for the next eighteen or twenty-one years.

By the time Mitch pulled into his driveway, he wanted nothing more than to hurry into his house, grab a beer, and take the longest, coolest shower in the history of

Texas. But the minute he climbed out of his car, Jenny stuck her head out from behind her kitchen door—making even temporary escape impossible.

"Hurry, McCord. You're just in time to feed your daughter her dinner!"

Chapter Four

There went his plans for a beer.

With a sigh that came out more like a groan, Mitch put his flight bag, hat and jacket inside the doorway of his house before striding across to Jenny's. He thought she had a heck of a nerve to sound so cheerful.

"My, Grandma," she drawled as he topped the stairs, "what glowering eyes you have. What's the matter? Have a bad day?"

"No thanks to you."

She looked sincerely surprised at that. "Don't tell me that you're still bristling because I had to keep our phone conversation short?"

"Short? It was virtually nonexistent."

"Because you happened to call at a bad moment for me."

"Join the club. In the past twenty-four hours *all* my moments have been bad." No sooner were the words out than he realized he might have been speaking to more than Jenny, but as he entered the house, he saw that except for the baby, she was alone.

He crossed to the kitchen table and leaned over the basket. His daughter was awake and gazing around the room, her blue eyes wide. Despite the tension between Jenny and him, seeing Mary again brought home all the surprise and awe that he'd felt watching her sleep last night.

"Excuse me, but I think we need to get a few things straight," Jenny said from behind him. "Now I am completely in sympathy with what a shock this situation has been for you. At the same time, I would appreciate it if you would remember that *you* got yourself into this situation by participating in unsafe sex, and that *you* came to me, a working woman, asking for help."

"I didn't say—"

"Oh, yes, you have, buster! You pushed every button you could to make me feel sorry for you, and you had every intention of using me for your own convenience."

No one liked to hear the truth put so accurately, and he was no exception. "I was desperate, knocked for a loop!"

"You're telling me."

"Will you let me finish? What I was about to say is that no matter how desperate I was, I wouldn't have left the baby with just anyone. She's here because I trust you."

"Be still my heart. I still have a business to run. I had every right to do what I did in order to save my product."

"If you were holding Mary at that moment, would you have dropped her to take care of some jam?" he snapped.

She drew herself erect and placed her hands on her hips. "It was *chutney,* you epicurean blockhead, and how dare you suggest I would hurt that child! If that's the way you feel, why don't you just take her and go do a better job yourself!"

"Great idea! I will!"

Of course their sharp voices made the baby cry, and that made Mitch feel more helpless and angry. But Jenny had punctured a hole in his pride, and he saw no way around it. His blood boiling, he snatched up the basket and stalked from the house.

"Oh, that— *Oh...*" Jenny's face crumbled into a combination wince and grimace.

"Well, that was interesting. If you two represent today's young people's idea of courting, I'm glad I'm an old woman."

Jenny spun around to find her grandmother standing in the kitchen doorway, and in a flash her fighting spirit was back again. "Don't group me in the same category as that... thankless *man!* Did you hear what he said to me?"

"I did, and no doubt so did Agnes, Minny, and Ethel, wherever those three are nestled to discuss this afternoon's news."

The mention of the town's worst gossips didn't faze Jenny for an instant. "I had a right to get upset. He was being insensitive and single-minded."

"You provoked him."

"I did not!"

Fiona went to the stove and turned off the fire beneath the pot warming the baby's formula. "I heard the whole thing, remember? Both this morning when he phoned, and just now."

That was the less-than-fun part about living together. Jenny never got to embellish a story, unlike her theatrical and creative kin who claimed full dibs to the right. But that didn't mean she intended to wear the halo people kept foisting on her, either.

"Well, I've been thinking about things since he dropped that bomb yesterday, and I decided I'd been too..."

"Neighborly?" Fiona offered.

Jenny gave her a droll look. "To say the least. The man had a baby with another woman, for pity's sake! What was I thinking to accept that as if it were nothing?"

"You're absolutely right. The bum should have asked you first if it was all right."

"*Gran.*" What was with her? "This morning you thought I'd lost my mind for agreeing to help him."

"That was then. This is now. If you're going to do it, then help him. Don't play games when he's already so confused. It's a miracle he can concentrate on flying."

That went to her conscience like a laser. "I'm not playing games." However, when her grandmother gave her a mild look, she had to acknowledge the words sounded less than truthful, even to her. She spread her arms wide. "Okay, so I hate what he's done! Why couldn't he have been spending all this time wanting me?"

"Because until today he thought you were a lovely and sweet girl."

That sounded about as interesting as molded cheese. Nice girls stayed home. They got used. "No more vanilla ice cream for me. I'm sorry if this makes me seem impulsive and erratic to him. But I have my own self-respect to juggle."

"Do tell? Then you believe it's in good taste to torment a man when he's just been delivered the back of life's hand?"

"Phooey. His past caught up with him, that's all."

"It's neither your place nor your temperament to punish."

"Who's punishing! Besides, if there's one thing Mitch McCord knows how to do, it's rebound."

Her grandmother crossed back to her and took hold of her hands. "Darling. I think it's time you decide what you want. Sending the man mixed signals on top of what he's dealing with will only make things more difficult for you. And it'll turn him into someone less capable of commitment than before. No one asked you to pine away for the man all these years. That was your choice, just as it was yours to all but invite him to reach out to you. Now he has. What are you doing about it?"

"I could probably think of something if you sounded more like Cinderella's fairy godmother than Vince Lombardi." Jenny felt an irrational urge to pout. Settling for a deep breath, she gave her grandmother a rueful look. "I *did* have to hang up, but... I guess I could have enjoyed it less than I did."

This time the older woman threw back her head and laughed. "That sounds more like you."

Jenny squeezed the older woman's strong but wrinkled hands. "What do I do, Gran?"

"Accept George Humphrey's invitation to go to the concert he told you about in church last Sunday."

"You can't be serious!"

"Just because I defended Friendly Skies doesn't mean I'm on his side. On the contrary, I'm more convinced than ever that he's all wrong for you."

"While you're at it, would you mind noticing that George is too *old* for me?"

"Age is relative." But her grandmother could, apparently, see the stress this was causing her. "At least give the object of your obsession time to cool down. Then you can go talk to him."

"With my luck he won't even answer the door."

"He'll have to. He left most of the baby's things here."

Including the infant's dinner. Jenny thought of how she'd upset Mary and a new wave of chagrin swept over her. "Maybe I should go now."

"Later. He has food over there. Keeping himself busy with that little one is the best remedy you could ask for right now."

Reassured, Jenny hugged her grandmother. "For a person who doesn't approve of him, you sure are being helpful, not to mention fair."

"That's why I'm obliged to warn you that I intend to invite George to dinner soon."

"*Why?*"

"Well, he may be too young for me, but he does have tickets to see Tony Bennett."

With a laugh, Jenny nodded. "Fair enough."

Jenny managed to delay going next door until after eight o'clock. By then her grandmother was entrenched in the living room watching her gossip shows on the TV cable channels, too preoccupied to offer any last-minute advice or peek at her from the kitchen win-

dow. Giving her freshly brushed hair a pat, Jenny slung
the baby's tote bag over her shoulder and hurried across
to Mitch's house, the skirt of her sunflower sundress
flaring around her legs.

He didn't respond to her knock, and she hesitated
ringing the doorbell, in case the baby had already settled down for the evening. Upon trying the doorknob,
she found it open, and poked her head inside.

"Hello... Mitch?"

Seconds later he appeared in the kitchen doorway,
barefoot, shirtless and, except for the slacks of his pilot's uniform, looking much as he did when he mowed
the lawn. For a moment her mind went blank as to why
she'd come over. Not even the weight of the tote bag on
her shoulder helped to jump-start her thoughts. All she
could focus on was that he looked virile and sexy, and
almost too good to be true.

"Could we, um, talk?"

He seemed to need a minute to consider that. "I don't
want to argue anymore. Not just because the baby's
sleeping. I just don't."

"Me, neither. That's why I'm here. I came to apologize."

"It's not necessary."

"It is to me."

He studied her in silence for several more seconds,
and then beckoned her the rest of the way inside. Jenny
let the storm door ease shut behind her, while taking in
the fact that soft, soothing music played in the background; that except for the faint smell of formula, he'd
probably not cooked for himself; that the emotions
emanating from him were more wary than angry.

"I brought this, too." She let the strap of the tote bag slip from her shoulder and set the thing on the kitchen table. "I figured you might need it."

"I thought about coming over for it, but I kept changing my mind."

"You were angry."

He appeared uncomfortable with that word. "Maybe not all I was feeling was due to what you did or said. Although I will admit I wanted it to be. Wanted someone else to blame. I needed some quiet time to figure out what's going on inside me."

That was about the scariest thing she'd ever heard. Jenny clasped her hands together, searching for something wise or witty to say. How ironic that what usually came easy didn't now. She felt as tongue-tied as if this was the first time they'd met. But in a way, it was. If she wanted Mitch to take her seriously, as something more than his neighbor, she needed to change how they approached each other from here on out.

"At first I wanted to come right over, but then I realized I needed some space and time, too," she told him, hoping he'd give her the chance to say more.

He nodded. "I suppose after all these years, my asking you for help sounded kind of hypocritical, didn't it?"

"No. Maybe desperate. And sweet, in a way." If she was going to be this honest, she decided she might as well go the rest of the way. "I was grateful you came to me, Mitch. In a way, I suppose I've been waiting my entire life for you to need me. I'm afraid I let myself get too full of those feelings."

He didn't seem to know how to respond to that. He glanced around as if realizing they were in his house and that it was up to him to do something. Gesturing over his shoulder, he said, "The baby's asleep. Would you like a glass of wine or something?"

Wine. She didn't often drink, but the idea of sitting down, sharing a glass of wine over intimate conversation, spawned appealing pictures in Jenny's mind. "That would be lovely. Thanks." She would be careful to sip it. If he was doing the talking, he would never know that she already felt too light-headed to risk drinking much alcohol.

Mitch took an opened green bottle from the refrigerator and pulled out the ornate cork. Then he took a long-stemmed glass from a nearby cupboard and half filled it.

"Thank you," Jenny said, accepting it from him.

"I'm having coffee in there." He gestured to his living room.

Coffee. Of course he wouldn't join her. He still had to fly again tomorrow, and just who was going to take care of Mary in his absence?

She led the way into the next room, but ignored the music, the cozy, masculine chairs, and the picture window that would have given her a place to retreat in order to collect her thoughts. She simply stopped in the middle of the room and decided to get to the point before she lost her nerve.

"Look, Mitch—"

"Jenny, I know I—"

Like her, Mitch stopped and smiled at the awkward start. "Go ahead," she told him.

"No, you go ahead."

Of all the times for him to resort to behaving like a gentleman. It would be so much easier to hear what he had to say first. "Why don't you start? Most of this is about you, anyway."

"I'm not so sure about that."

"What do you mean?" Clarity took its time, leaving her feeling several paces behind his thoughts. "You're the parent."

"Alleged parent."

He said that so dryly that she could find a chuckle for the humor behind it. "Whatever. In any case, it's more than being just the baby-sitter."

"You're more than simply the baby-sitter."

"I am?"

"Aren't you?"

She hadn't even had a sip of the wine yet and she had already lost track of the conversation. Opting for reverse psychology, she took a healthy sip and tried to respond to his question as honestly as she could. "It's no secret that I've wanted you to notice me for ages, Mitch. Suffice it to say that maybe I should have faced reality a long time ago, and got on with my life. Maybe I'm here to tell you that I'm sorry for being such an albatross, and that I've finally gotten the message."

"You're giving up."

Of all the responses he could have made... Jenny scratched at a sudden itch at her temple. "Why do I feel as if you haven't handed me my script yet? This is totally unlike you, McCord."

"Yeah, I guess. But the Jenny Stevens you introduced me to today is a different person than the one who's been peeking at me through her blinds and offering shy invitations for the longest time." As she opened her mouth to speak, he held up his hand. "I know I have no right to be receptive to that Jenny, but despite the state of my life right now, I like her."

"You do?"

"She's funny, fresh, and annoyingly sexy."

"Annoyingly?" Jenny took one more sip of her wine before putting it down on the coffee table to avoid spilling it. The man certainly knew how to get to the core of her emotions. "Would you like to explain that?"

"Not really. I don't even like having this conversation."

"Then why are we?"

"Because I can't see us going on as we are." Mitch crossed his arms and began looking more than a little uncomfortable. "I'll admit I've done everything in my power to dissuade you from paying attention to me, even to the point of annoying you."

If it was anyone else, Jenny would think the man had one super ego, but she knew Mitch didn't have to pretend or make false assumptions now. "But now you have a daughter and need reliable help to care for her."

"It's not so simple or mercenary."

She would have been a liar if she claimed that didn't interest her. "Go on."

"Jenny, I can't deny I haven't taken the easy way out of dealing with relationships. That message was brought home to me more than once in the past few days, but today in particular. And I wouldn't blame you if you said you wanted nothing more to do with me."

"But..."

"You set off strange, unexpected alarm bells inside me. I keep trying to deny them, to ignore them, but that just makes it worse."

"Alarm bells are rarely a positive thing."

"For you, they wouldn't be."

Mercy. That was a provocative statement, and suddenly she wanted a moment to collect her wits. Jenny moistened her lips. "Could we talk about your day for a moment? Obviously something happened that's challenged your perceptions yet again.''

He ran his hand over his chest, and started, as if just realizing his state of undress. "Maybe I'd better go put on something.''

"You're fine the way you are." Perfect, in fact. "Just tell me."

Mitch recrossed his arms over his chest and made an overlong perusal of the area on either side of Jenny's shoulders. "Savannah isn't going to be easy to locate. Either she's left the Los Angeles area or she's got an unlisted number. What's more, no one has come forward to claim the baby."

"That doesn't come as any real surprise, does it?"

"No. But as I was returning to the plane after those calls, I met someone I used to date. The opportunity to . . . try again was there."

Barely able to suppress a gulp, Jenny nodded, hoping she looked more contemplative than jealous. "Fate can have a strange sense of humor sometimes."

"That's the understatement of the week. The point is, I realized I didn't want to. Go out again. With that person, I mean."

As much as she wanted to know why, Jenny refused to ask the question. Whatever he wanted her to know at this point was his choice. She would make her own decisions thereafter.

"Because of you, Jen. Because it would have felt as if I was cheating on you."

Whatever she'd expected to hear, it was a good deal less than this. Small wonder that her world did a dizzying three-hundred-sixty-degree spin and her heart pounded at an insane tempo. "Why?"

His expression told her that he had no answer, at least not one he was ready to verbalize.

"Never mind," she told him. "When my parents died, it took me a good while to recognize that in the beginning, the only way my grandmother could handle her grief was through silence. I was so caught up in my need to talk that I thought no one else's counted as much. It's a bad habit to fall into, and we do it because the people who love us let us indulge in ourselves."

Mitch smiled. "See. I struggle to tell you, and you already have the answers."

That made Jenny grimace. "Please. Don't put me on a pedestal. At this stage I won't just fall off, I'll jump from sheer nausea."

That earned her a perplexed look. "You're turning into one mystery after another, Jen. And that's been hitting home loud and clear."

"Okay... you're ready to acknowledge that I have a brain. Where does that leave us?"

"With you being a terrific lady and me being one scared jerk."

This was not a scenario that had been covered by any soap opera her grandmother had quoted philosophy from, or a situation that any friend had relayed to her. She thought of her best source of expertise on love and relationships. However, like everyone else these days, her friend Valerie Kincaid had made Jenny conscious of the fragility in the male-female cycle of bonding. Valerie and Lucas had been married for several years and of all people, Jenny had believed they had the "forever after" thing down pat. However, a few weeks ago Valerie had admitted that even she and Lucas were not quite the picture of harmony people thought. With a black cloud like that hanging over romance's head, who had a right to hope for anything from this confusing situation?

"Look, McCord," she began with a self-conscious laugh, "you don't have to do this. We're neighbors. I think your baby is adorable. And despite my behavior earlier, I am willing and able to help you. That's all we need to cover if you like."

"But what if I'm confused about what I like?"

Oh, brother.

Jenny drew a long breath and wished she had time to call Val. "Then take a few days to think about it." She began edging toward the door, escape sounding particularly good to her. "Why don't you call me when you come to at least one or two tentative solutions about Mary and we'll discuss them."

Before she got to the door, Mitch had circled her and was blocking her path. To her amazement, he took hold of her upper arms and gazed deeply into her eyes.

"Maybe we should discuss one or two things now."

Then he kissed her.

Unprepared, for several seconds Jenny stared into the face so close to hers before realizing this was really happening. After all these years of wishing and dreaming.... And wasn't it just like her, she thought, closing her eyes with chagrin, that her slow-witted response was to simply stand there like a piece of plywood?

No, you don't, Jenny Stevens. You've waited too long for this!

With a happy sigh, she wrapped her arms around his neck and began kissing him back.

How strong he felt, and how warm and solid. She was almost tempted to open her eyes again to fully savor the moment, except that Mitch was moving his hands into her hair and slanting his mouth over hers for a more determined claiming. His hungrier kiss made it all but impossible for her to think, let alone rationalize clearly. Within seconds, every other kiss she'd ever experienced was reduced to being as stimulating as an obligatory handshake.

Before long her stomach clenched from a craving that had nothing to do with food. Yet she resisted yielding to necessity, wanting the moment to last for fear it might never happen again. In the end it was Mitch who saved her by tearing his mouth from hers to explore her cheek, her temple, and her chin.

"Sweet heaven, you taste good," he whispered against her feverish skin.

His praise thrilled her almost as much as his caresses did. "So do you."

That had him seeking her mouth again, and this time he nibbled at her, coaxing her to give him full access. With the blood rushing to her head, she yielded gladly, knowing she couldn't have resisted if she wanted to. Then the kiss became a seduction, more gentle nips, sexy strokes of his tongue, and suckling kisses.

By the time he lifted his head, they were both breathing as if they'd sprinted around the New Hope High School track—and more than a few times!

"Man, oh, man..."

"What?"

"This is exactly what I was afraid of."

Unwilling to be anything less than honest, Jenny replied, "I'm not sorry. I don't want you to be, either." She touched his strong, slightly whisker-rough chin with her index finger. "You're a good kisser."

"You're the one." But that comment came with a frown. "Who taught you?"

Now that was amusing—New Hope's own Casanova being jealous of *her* limited experience. Smiling, she leaned back to bat her lashes at him. "McCord, I do believe it is ungallant to ask a lady such a question."

"Especially when it's me doing the asking," he muttered, gathering her close again. "But damn, Jen, did what just happened affect you the way it did me?"

She knew she was being greedy, but she loved watching him as he dealt with his emotions. Besides, a woman would have to be crazy to grow tired of listening to him say lovely things to her. "What did you feel?"

"Blown away. Breathless. Perfect."

"It was...something."

"Yeah, something else. Now you know why I've been trying to stay away from you."

"You couldn't have known."

"I knew. Suspected. Chemistry's a weird thing."

As his eyes grew almost smoky with renewed interest, Jenny moistened her lips. "So now what?"

"I don't know. It would be a lie to pretend I don't want you in my life, Jenny. I want you in Mary's, as well."

"Why do I hear a but?"

Concern added lines between his dark blond eyebrows. "You know why. It's shades of the same old argument. We're neighbors, and I'm not the kind of guy you should be getting involved with."

"I don't care how many women you've dated."

"That's only part of the issue. You're too good a person to be trifled with."

Her humor took on a wicked twist and she smiled impishly at him. "Are you thinking about trifling with me?"

"Dammit, you know what I mean. You deserve promises. I'm not about to make any."

"I don't recall asking you for a commitment," she replied with a lift of her chin.

He ignored that. "It wouldn't be fair to you. And on top of everything else, I haven't even had a chance to get used to the idea that I may be raising a child."

He needed time, that's all. And considering the depth of the passion that had exploded between them, she was more than willing to give it to him, to give things a chance to evolve at a natural pace. "You haven't succeeded in scaring me away yet, Mitch McCord, and you aren't going to now. So why don't you just try not worrying so much and take each day as it comes."

He stroked her lower lip with his thumb. "God, forgive me for being a selfish lug, but I'm going to do that. *And* take advantage of your generosity. With one stipulation."

"What's that?" she asked, wishing he would stop talking and kiss her again.

"Let's make a pact to take things really slowly. Kissing is good, but anything more is definitely off-limits. If I get . . . carried away, I want you to help me cool things down pronto. Agreed?"

"And if I get carried away?" she asked, indulging in the luxury of exploring the golden hair sprinkled across the broad expanse of his tanned chest.

He sucked in a sharp breath. "Jen . . . honey, I didn't last six months in the Boy Scouts, so you'll just have to be the disciplinarian for both of us, okay?"

If he thought she had that kind of endurance, he had one big surprise coming. Fortunately, before she could tell him so, he kissed her again.

Chapter Five

"There she is. Get the pew behind them."

"She doesn't look any different, Aggie."

"Of course she doesn't look any different, you ninny. It's not her baby!"

For her part, Jenny found the awkward shuffling and whispers going on behind her amusing, but seated beside her, her grandmother bristled with indignation.

"You'd think some people would have a little more respect for being in a house of worship," she whispered loudly out of the side of her mouth.

Jenny knew the comment was really for the three busybodies behind her, and held back a grin by bowing her head over the baby. Mary slept peacefully in her arms, despite the spirited psalm being played by the organist.

When Jenny had offered to keep the baby overnight because Mitch had been scheduled to participate in a charity tennis tournament in Dallas today, she'd known appearing at church with Mary would raise eyebrows, especially since news always spread quickly through the small North Texas community. But Minny, Agnes and Ethel were ever on the search for new or expanded news. Jenny thought of them as the Three Musketeers of Gossip.

"They're just curious," she whispered back to her grandmother. "And I don't mind."

What concerned her more was that she could see Valerie entering the church, and despite waving, Jenny couldn't get her attention. Val was dressed as lovely as ever, but she was very much alone in her pew on the far side of the church. Did that mean she and Lucas had quarreled again? Jenny willed her friend to look her way, but once settled, Val opened her bible and didn't glance up until Reverend Borden took his place behind the podium.

That wasn't to say that church didn't prove a pleasant and rejuvenating experience. Reverend Borden's sermon was on virtues and the need for more patience in this stressful day and age. But as Jenny suspected, she didn't need to reach for much patience with Mary—the baby proved a perfect angel throughout the service. By the time they rose to leave, Jenny's heart couldn't have been more filled with pride for the infant if she'd given birth to the child herself.

Of course, Jenny knew better than to hope she could get out of the church without a confrontation with the eager ladies behind her. Her grandmother muttered as much as she followed Jenny out into the aisle.

"Why, Jenny Stevens," Agnes gushed, placing a crocheted gloved hand to her flat bosom. She was always the leader and instigator of the group. "What precious tidbit do you have there?"

"Since when did your eyesight go bad, Agnes?" Jenny's grandmother snapped, glaring at the taller woman.

"I was only making polite conversation, Fiona. Since when did you get so sensitive? You have nothing to be ashamed of—that is, if rumor proves accurate."

"Humph," Fiona muttered. "And just who started those rumors?"

Knowing that if she didn't do something, her grandmother could happily butt heads with the Three Musketeers all day, Jenny spoke up. "This is Mary McCord, ladies. She's Mitch McCord's daughter and we're babysitting while he participates in a charity function."

"That's just like you, Jenny," Ethel said, beaming. "You're always doing such nice things for other people."

"When did little Mitchell McCord marry?" sweet, but slightly daffy Minny piped in.

Agnes elbowed the dainty woman. "*Little* Mitchell hasn't, Min. That's the point!" She then reached out to clasp Jenny by the wrist. "So how did all this come about, and who's the mother?"

Although she couldn't keep her eyes from twinkling with mischief, Jenny replied, "Oh, I imagine it happened the usual way, Agnes. Mitch isn't quite the type to frequent the town sperm bank. Isn't Mary adorable? Gran and I are always saying she has to be the most well-behaved baby in the history of babies."

"It sounds as if you're quite smitten, dear," Ethel piped in, as sharp-eyed and smooth as Agnes.

"Oh, I am. No doubt about it."

"But I don't believe I heard what you said about the mother, dear," Agnes interjected.

"That's because I didn't mention her, Agnes. It's Mitch's place to do that. Now if you'll excuse me, I'd really like to say hello to a friend before she leaves."

Confident that her grandmother could handle the trio, Jenny hurried across the church just in time to intercept Valerie as she tried to make her escape through a side door. Jenny caught hold of the shoulder strap on her friend's bag.

"Hey, stranger? What gives?"

"Jen . . . hi."

The weak response and overbright eyes confirmed Jenny's suspicions that all was not right. "Is something wrong?"

"Oh . . . no. How's it going?" Then her gaze focused on the small bundle in Jenny's arms. "My goodness, what's this?"

Had her friend been so out of it that she hadn't listened to any of the phone messages Jenny had left her? "This is Mary McCord."

"McCord . . . As in your neighbor, Mitch?"

Jenny nodded. "None other." She quickly capsulized the story for her friend.

"You poor thing," Valerie murmured, reaching across the baby to give her a belated but careful hug. "Are you okay with all this? Heaven knows, you look absolutely . . . glowing."

Because it was Val who asked, Jenny found it easier to be direct. "Surprisingly, I'm okay. Granted, I'd have been a good deal happier if this was *my* baby, but seeing how torn Mitch has been over the situation—"

"You and your Mitch." Valerie sighed, her expression gentling and yet growing more sad than ever. "This goes above and beyond the call of good-neighborliness *or* unrequited love, Jen."

"But he cares," Jenny insisted. "This shock has really spawned a change in him."

"You think so?"

"Anyone can see it. He has a clarity and sensitivity that either wasn't there before or that he'd denied. Oh, I'm not pretending he's changed completely. I wouldn't want that even if it was possible. But, Val, do you know what? He admitted the other day that he's always had feelings for me."

"I never doubted that. He worked too hard to deflect your attention. But he has an odd way of exposing his feelings now—not to mention pretty bad timing."

This was nothing Jenny hadn't heard before. "He's admitted as much, Val. And he hasn't tried to underplay the seriousness about anything that's happened."

"Then why the years of being so standoffish, even rude?"

"You know what I told you about his background. His parents' ugly divorce, the way they used him as a pawn to control and hurt each other, as if *he* had no feelings and needs of his own. He doesn't trust in his ability to overcome his past fear and resentment to be a fair and whole partner to someone."

"Marriage is difficult enough without taking on those handicaps. You deserve more, Jenny."

"No. In any case, I want Mitch. What's more, I believe I can help him, because I've seen and understand what he's been through. I know what he needs."

Valerie's smile was forced. "I wish I could agree, but I'm afraid you might be setting yourself up for major disappointment. At least promise me you'll take your time, Jen. Make sure you two are truly on the same wavelength before you risk your heart completely."

Once again Jenny felt an overwhelming sadness underscoring her friend's words. "Why are you acting like this? Don't tell me it's simply about me and my dreams, either. It's you. Where's Lucas these days? And why haven't you returned my calls? What's going on, Val?"

Valerie looked away, a flash of poignant pain making her eyes bright with tears. "Explaining that would take more than a thirty-second sound bite, pal of mine. Can I take a rain check? I really do have to go."

As Valerie left, Jenny stood there, amazed. Val had never been one to cut any conversation short, usually enjoying their chats as much as she did. In fact until recently they were known to touch base by phone or in person nearly every day.

Jenny reunited with her grandmother and as they were settling into the van they used as a delivery vehicle and to pick up supplies, she voiced her concern. "I'm worried about Valerie."

"Everyone has problems these days." Fiona reached over to pat her on the shoulder. "I'm more concerned with the gossip going on around town about Mitch. Well, you and Mitch. You just make sure to ignore those female barracudas, especially that Agnes. That woman's always taking two and two and getting five out of things. I told her just because we don't want to discuss the baby's maternity, doesn't mean Mitch got the child as a result of some sperm bank foolery or something more outlandish."

"Oh, my. I didn't know the stories were getting that creative." But as Jenny thought about the congregation's general attitude, she decided that despite her grandmother's fretting, most people had been rather nice, once she'd explained she was just baby-sitting and didn't know many details herself.

She drove home with the mid-August sun illuminating a rejuvenated North Texas countryside. It had rained again in the past few days, and the ripe-wheat color that had been taking over the landscape due to the heat and dryness was yielding to a greener tint. Jenny hoped things would stay moist enough for them to enjoy a little fall color. They could never compete with the golden aspens in Colorado or the yellow and orange maples and oaks in New England; but when nature was benevolent, the flowering pear trees resembled Olympic torches lining streets and surrounding homes and office buildings, while the maples and sweet gum trees provided seasonal accent in rural areas.

As Jenny drove, her grandmother chattered aimlessly, not expecting a response, but merely venting her thoughts. That allowed Jenny to follow her own musings...so much so that she was slow to realize, upon their return home, that a strange car stood in Mitch's driveway.

She pulled into her driveway, her heart leaping into her throat out of concern. "Who could that be?"

"Where's Mitch's car?" her grandmother asked right afterward.

Jenny was about to tell her that surely Mitch had already left for the tournament when he emerged from his house and walked over to open the driver's door for her.

"Well, hi," she began. "Aren't you supposed to be gone by now? And what's happened to your car?"

Beneath his ever-neatly-trimmed mustache, his mouth twisted into a grimace. "Would you believe the water pump broke as I pulled out of the driveway?"

"Oh, no!"

"Don't I always say those fancy cars are nothing more than expensive toys?" Her grandmother pointed at Mitch, her silver charm bracelet tinkling. "You tell me I'm wrong now, Friendly Skies!"

Mitch gave Jenny a look that said he wouldn't consider it. Then he added, "The good news is that the dealership was great about picking it up and bringing over a sedan."

"Well, you are a devoted customer." She didn't think he kept any one car for more than sixteen months before turning it in for a newer model. She followed him around the van and watched him unstrap Mary from her car seat. "Wait a minute, what are you doing? If you're late, you should be—"

"It's all right. I was going to go early just to watch a few matches. But while I was waiting for the car and tow truck—" he added, pausing to kiss the baby's forehead "—I had an idea."

He gave her ideas, too. From the moment she'd spotted him in his white knit shirt and shorts, and the headband that would keep his sun-gold hair out of his eyes as he charged around the tennis court, her heart had been beating like crazy. But since their enlightening talk a few days ago, work and getting used to having a baby in their lives had kept them both preoccupied. There hadn't been much opportunity to explore their long-suppressed and evolving feelings. When added to the pressure of being under the watchful eye of her grandmother, Jenny concluded that it was a miracle either one of them could *pretend* to feel normal.

"An idea about what?" Jenny asked. He had sounded upbeat, but if he was going to tell her that he'd changed his mind about her having so much time with the baby, she would simply cry.

"Would you like to come along?"

"To the tournament?" she asked, sure she'd misunderstood.

"I have a couple of company tickets to the airline's private box. You'll be out of the sun, and there'll be all sorts of food and refreshments."

"But . . . the baby?"

"I can watch the baby," her grandmother announced.

"Thanks for the offer, but I thought we'd take her with us," Mitch replied. "As well behaved as she is, she'll probably sleep through the whole thing, and it would give me an opportunity to show her off." He focused on Jenny with an intentness that willed her to see only him. "I know you won't know anyone there, but I'll be with you for a while before I play."

Jenny's irrepressible humor wouldn't leave her alone. "Is this a date, McCord?"

He swallowed. His gaze swung to her grandmother before meeting hers again. "Well . . . yeah. It's time, don't you think?"

Sure, but she still couldn't believe it. "This is awfully nice, but have you considered how your friends and co-workers will react? People are going to think . . . the obvious."

"No, I don't think so. Enough of them know that Mary's mother isn't around. Once I introduce you as my neighbor, the rest will know better than to jump to conclusions."

"Heaven save me from male logic," her grandmother muttered from behind her.

Mitch looked truly confused. "What do you mean?"

Jenny smiled and touched his cheek to reassure him. "Ignore her. She's hasn't had her lunch yet and she's getting light-headed.'' Then she glanced over her shoulder and shot her grandmother a speaking look.

"Excuse me for having an opinion," Fiona replied. "I'll just stand here and get heatstroke."

Despite her grandmother's sarcasm, Jenny couldn't be more excited. Imagine spending an entire afternoon with Mitch! Then she glanced down at her old-fashioned ivory lace gown with the full skirt. It was nice, but hardly appropriate attire for a sporty tennis match. If only she had something crisp and sexy and white like people wore at the matches she'd glimpsed on TV.

"You look wonderful," he told her, apparently reading her expression. "But I could change the baby's diaper while you got into something you may feel is more comfortable."

She did have a coral sundress with a swirly skirt that she had yet to wear. She had bought it on impulse during a brief shopping trip to Dallas with Valerie earlier in the year. Valerie had said that with her hair brushed to full glossiness around her shoulders and some strappy sandals, she could hold her own in it anywhere.

Then she shot her grandmother a look of appeal. "Sure you don't mind?"

"I offered to take care of the baby, didn't I? But if he wants her to go along, go. It's just as well since I was thinking about going over to see Agnes and finish giving her a piece of my mind anyway."

"I'm going to pretend you didn't say that." Facing Mitch again, Jenny said, "Give me five minutes. Ten at the most!"

"Having second thoughts?"

"No!" As her question broke into his thoughts,

Mitch reached over to touch Jenny's cheek. "I'm fine, and you look beautiful."

She knew the outfit was flattering to her autumn coloring, and that the dress's cinched waist did accent her slimness, but compliments always helped, especially when they came from Mitch. "Thanks. I still can't believe you invited me."

"I should have asked you Friday, but I didn't think you'd be interested. You've never said anything about liking tennis."

"To be honest, I've never wanted to play it myself, but I admire anyone who's good at the game. Those trophies I saw in your house tell me that you're better than good."

He didn't exactly shrug, but he was aware one needed more than talent to achieve a career in the sport. "At one time I guess I could have tried to make it professionally, but then I caught my mother with my tennis instructor."

"Oh, no! While she was still married to your father?"

Mitch managed an indifferent nod, but gripped the plush sedan's steering wheel tightly as he remembered his anger, and later his bitterness. "After that I refused to practice. By the time I realized I wasn't hurting anyone but myself, I'd lost too much valuable time."

"I wish I'd known," Jenny told him, her voice soft. "Now that I think back, I seem to remember how much more remote and quiet you became."

"Sullen," Mitch said with a crooked smile.

"But you discovered flying instead. And hasn't that proved to be your great love?"

"In a way." Until recently, he'd believed he'd lost the ability to feel too deeply. "Actually, it's more like a philosophy with me, the way t'ai chi ch'uan is to other people."

"Now there's a perspective that never crossed my mind."

"You thought maybe it was a speed thing because of the kind of car I like to drive?"

"It certainly would fit the image."

Man, he had done a good job at fooling her. And maybe there had been an ounce or two of truth to the idea. Once. Mitch exited from Central Expressway to the LBJ Freeway, which would take them toward Las Colinas where the event was being held.

"I love flying because it clears my head of... nonsense," he said, struggling to explain. "Makes me feel free."

"Is freedom so important to you?"

"At times it's been all but imperative." Especially when his parents were tearing each other apart like rabid dogs. Back then freedom had meant silence, an escape from emotional pain and disappointment. An independence he thought would guarantee him emotional safety. How wrong he'd been about that, as well. "But I've never used the sky for an adrenaline fix, not when I have a couple hundred people in my care."

"That theory doesn't extend to your car, does it?"

He chuckled to himself, liking her gentle teasing. "Ah...well, I *am* human." Then he adjusted the rear-view mirror to check on the sleeping bundle of pink in the car seat he'd removed from Jenny's van while he waited for her. "However, I can safely say that just as with flying, there are things I won't risk."

With a contented sigh, Jenny settled back against the leather seat. "I didn't think so."

They drove for a moment or two in contented silence. Traffic was light compared to a weekday, but Mitch still had to watch for those who drove as if they had to make El Paso by nightfall. In the distance, the downtown Dallas skyline shimmered like a futuristic movie set.

"At the risk of blowing this date before it begins, I was wondering if you'd had any success with the private detective you hired?"

He might have felt a bit sensitive about such an inquiry from her before; however, he believed she had a right to ask now. "No, I haven't. I've been thinking that if I don't hear from him by Monday, I'll call him. Waiting is the pits."

"You have to be feeling as if you're dangling from some high wire."

"Something like that. Mary and I are beginning to bond. She's beginning to recognize me. I want things explained and resolved. For all of our sakes." He glanced her way. "You see, I'm not unaware of what an uncomfortable situation this is for you, too."

Jenny sighed. "In a way it is, sure. But, Mitch, would we be talking like this, would we be together, if there was no Mary?"

He couldn't lie to her. "I don't know. On the other hand, you have to admit you are one unignorable lady, Jen."

"I've been telling the man this for ages," she whispered to the roof of the car as she clasped her hands under her chin. "Thank you for letting it sink in before I started going gray and losing my teeth."

"Nut." Mitch laughed, but he was charmed, too, and more and more glad that he'd followed the impulse to break down and invite Jenny.

He broke another promise to himself when he finally parked outside the country club. Before they had to wake the baby, he released his seat belt, murmured, "Wait a second," to Jenny, and took her lips with his.

He relished her surprise, as much as he did the subtle tremor that ran through her. Most of all he enjoyed the way she recovered and leaned into him. Everything was so much more real with her compared to the performance he'd often settled for from other women. Although tempted to tell her that, he resisted, not wanting to remind her of the man he'd been.

"What was that for?" Jenny murmured when he finally eased back, just enough so he could lightly rub his nose against hers.

"I was hoping you'd bring me even more luck than you already have."

"Oh, dear . . . I hope you're not confusing me with that curvy blonde that comes out of a bottle."

He smiled as her words tickled his mustache. "What you have is far more potent. Sweet."

"Ugh." She made a face. "Why can't I be seen as sexy and beguiling for once?"

"You're sexy enough." He took hold of her fingers and pressed a kiss into her palm. "If you get any sexier I'm not going to be able to get out of this car without embarrassing myself."

"Oh."

The emotions that flickered across her face were adorable, and *yes,* damned sexy. Mitch wished like heck that they were back at his place, where he could stretch her out on his couch, or better yet, his bed, slip the feminine straps of her dress off her creamy shoulders and taste every inch of skin he exposed. What a sanity saver when the baby roused!

"We're spoiling her," Jenny said with a sigh. "We're all so eager to hold her that she's getting to where she'll only sleep when she feels motion." With one last, longing glance at his mouth, she eased her hand out of his and reached for her door handle.

Once Mitch had decided on bringing Jenny and Mary, he didn't spend a good deal of thought about what kind of reception they would get. In typical fashion, he assumed he would "handle things." What he forgot to consider was that he'd never seen Jenny in a social environment. Up to her elbows in berries, wilting from too many hours in a steamy kitchen, feverish and feisty from wrestling with a dying lawn mower... yes, he'd witnessed that side of her. But he'd let himself forget that he'd never experienced her dressed like a princess and emanating a more sophisticated, slightly reserved sexuality. He discovered he was ill prepared for having her pull the emotional rug out from under him.

Chapter Six

"Mitch! You found her?"

He managed to cover his wince, but Mitch could have shoved Neil Dennison into one of the arrangements of tropical plants for his big mouth. However, before he could straighten out Neil and the several other people who'd heard his co-worker's cheerful declarations and were heading their way, Jenny stepped forward and offered her hand.

"Hello, I'm Jennifer Stevens, Mitch's neighbor. I care for Mary when Mitch is flying."

His friend recovered well. Mitch decided it was because Jenny's warm smile could make anyone forget they'd been an insensitive jerk.

"Jennifer, one of my favorite names." Neil took her hand in both of his, and held on to it as he beamed down at the baby. "That little one looks as if she's in good hands. Does Mitch know how lucky he is to have found you?"

"Well, since I was never lost, I'm not sure."

"Good for you, Jennifer," a petite brunette said with a laugh as she joined them. "I'm Bonnie. This drooling, but harmless man is my husband, and I've been dying for a peek at this little sweetheart ever since I heard about her, so could I hold her while you take a break and enjoy a glass of champagne?"

"Neil and I fly together," Mitch said, smiling encouragingly at Jenny when she looked over her shoulder at him for approval. "And Bonnie is a veteran at child care. She has two of her own, a son and a daughter."

"You don't look old enough to have children," Jenny told Bonnie, easing her precious bundle into her arms.

"Oh, you doll! We're going to be wonderful friends."

In ones, twos, and threes they approached—administrative executives, crew members, a few VIPs. Mitch would have liked to think all the attention was because of his reputation as a damned good pilot with a superior flight record, as well as for being one of the airline's better known representatives in the tournament today. People did wish him luck, but he could tell it was always an afterthought, despite his having won this event two years in a row.

He then told himself that people were paying them an unusual amount of attention as a result of their natural curiosity about the baby. Someone quickly corrected him again.

"Your daughter is darling, Mitch. So well behaved. But I can't tell you how thrilled my husband is with meeting Jenny," said one VIP's wife. "I buy her products all the time. I'll drive clear across Dallas for them if my regular shop has sold out of a particular item, especially when we're expecting out-of-town guests. And

Stu's simply captivated with the lady. Says she has more business sense than his accountant and financial planner combined. Thank goodness she looks at you the way she does or I would forget I've been married too long to be jealous.''

"Do you suppose she would be interested in doing some advertising work?'' a guest Mitch didn't recognize asked shortly afterward, handing over a business card. "She has some elusive Mona Lisa quality about her that's classy and alluring, but at the same time unthreatening to women.''

By the time he had to leave to get ready for his game, Mitch noted that Jenny was now charming the president of the airline himself! Mitch signaled to her twice to no avail and wondered if either of them would notice if he went on court and played the entire game standing on his head.

Torn between being proud and speechless, he finally succeeded in catching her eye. She excused herself and, protecting Mary's head from the draft caused by the overhead fans, made her way to him.

Not about to risk being interrupted, he took hold of her elbow and led her out behind a potted palm for some privacy.

"Is it time?'' she asked him.

"Mmm. I was just wondering, though, if you'll be here when I get back, Miss Popularity.'' He loved the way her coffee-dark eyes glowed like cabochon, and there was a deeper peach tint to her cheeks that made her absolutely radiant.

"Didn't you want me to mingle and introduce your daughter to everyone?''

He had used that reason to convince her to come along, true, but it was only one part of the truth. There were other reasons, less defined and more provocative. He hadn't been able to tell her that he also wanted her company for selfish reasons: the reassurance of having someone around who knew his flaws better than anyone here, and had the innate generosity to overlook them. He wanted her around because of the aura of peacefulness he felt whenever he watched her with Mary. And yes, he asked her to come because it was getting damned difficult to ignore his growing attraction to her. But since their arrival, he'd seen a wholly different side of Jenny emerge, and that left him feeling more than a little bemused, not to mention amazed.

"Of course," he replied, beginning to think he'd do well not to draw too many conclusions about her. "But I had no idea you would be so good at it."

She lifted both finely arched eyebrows. "Why, McCord, I'm sure there's a compliment in there somewhere, only I'm not sure what it is."

"Ignore me." Unable to keep his hands to himself, he brushed a tendril of hair back from her face. "I think I'm just dealing with a unique case of jealousy."

"You?"

He didn't like the idea that she wasn't taking him seriously. "Yes, me. You have people all but eating out of your hand—not just because you're kind and gracious, but sharper than a hypodermic, too. I suppose I'm beginning to realize I don't know the first thing about you, Jen, and I don't feel good about being the last to figure that out."

"Poor baby." Another hint of laughter and mischief lit her thickly lashed eyes. "But guess what? Now's not the best time for you to worry about it. Didn't you say you had a match to play?"

He almost wished he didn't have to. Leaving her alone at this point didn't seem the wisest of ideas. He sighed. "To be continued. Agreed?"

"I'm not going anywhere. Well, except to change this sweetie's diaper before your match starts."

Mitch lifted her chin and met her twinkling gaze. "You enjoy seeing all this egg on my face, don't you?"

"Maybe a teensy bit."

"I guess I deserve that. Wish me luck?"

"You know I do."

"I'm feeling needy. Can you do a bit more?"

She rose on tiptoe and touched her lips to his. "Good luck."

"Maybe a little more?"

This time she took hold of his shirt and, careful to keep him from crushing the baby, tugged him down to her. The combination of tenderness and solemnity in her eyes added a poignancy to her next kiss that had him aching to reach for her. He had to satisfy himself by clinging hungrily to her lips.

"I'm in trouble," he murmured upon hearing his name mentioned over the loudspeakers.

"Sounds like it."

"Wonder how much trouble I'd get into if I told them that I've changed my mind. Wouldn't you much rather go find someplace cool and quiet where we could talk and watch the baby grab at butterflies?"

Jenny's sigh spoke volumes as she leaned back and adjusted his shirt. "It sounds heavenly, but it's a little late to back out now. People are counting on you, and regardless of what you say, you're not the type to back out once you've given your word."

She was proving to be one surprise after another. Mitch slid his hand under the thick silk of her hair to cup her neck. "Who are you, Jenny Stevens?"

"I'll give you a rain check to find out. But thanks for realizing you don't have a clue."

"Promise we'll get around to a full analysis later in the not-so-distant future?"

"Whenever you like. In the meantime, would you mind going out there and showing me how you really play this game?"

Jenny could have stood there all afternoon and half the night reliving the pleasure of watching Mitch walk away. He was every bit "the hunk" she'd heard some of the female guests call him behind his back. With those toned, tanned legs, slim hips and strong shoulders, he would win over the crowd and charm the media, even if he didn't win the match. She didn't want to miss a minute of it.

After changing Mary in the VIP lounge, she returned just as the last match ended. As the scoreboard changed and Mitch's name appeared along with that of a local TV anchorman, the crowd's enthusiasm rose.

"Come sit here, Jenny," Bonnie Dennison called to her from the front row of chairs arranged for those who were serious fans of the game. "I've saved you a seat."

She thanked the vivacious brunette and after settling on the cushioned chair with the baby, got out one of the cooled bottles of boiled water she'd been saving for Mary. Within seconds, Mary's tiny hands were clenching the bottle and she was sucking contentedly.

"For a novice, you're handling this awfully well," Bonnie told her, slipping on a pair of designer sunglasses that matched her blue-and-green silk jumpsuit.

"It's not difficult to do with a baby that's as easy to please as Mary." Jenny did shoot the other woman a wry smile. "Of course, it helps that as a teenager I earned the money to buy my first car by baby-sitting." She briefly told her about moving in with her grandmother after her parents' death, and the years spent as Mitch's neighbor.

"If it's any reassurance, Neil says he's been a different person in the past week ... and I have a feeling that it's not just due to the baby."

Jenny appreciated the comment. However, she felt uncomfortable discussing Mitch's situation—or theirs for that matter—with veritable strangers. "Actually, I've always sensed he had a tender and caring side. He simply needed a good enough reason to let it surface. The shock of discovering that he's responsible for another life is doing that."

Bonnie didn't appear to take any offense at the slightly formal reply. "I know when to keep my itchy nose out of other people's private affairs. Let me simply add that I hope he recognizes a good thing when he sees it. Now, tell me, have you seen him play before?"

"Never. But I have seen his trophies." Not wanting to expose how much she was looking forward to the match, Jenny was relieved to have Mary to focus on. Making sure the little piglet didn't overindulge provided considerable entertainment for both her and Bonnie. But finally the crowd announced the wait was over.

"Oh, there he is!" Bonnie pointed and burst into enthusiastic applause.

She explained that since this was a charity event, the rather reserved protocol expected of the audience wouldn't be enforced. Well behaved or not, Jenny listened to the crowd divide itself between Mitch and Bruce Paxton, the TV anchorman. Both accepted the whistles and humorous calls with grins and waves.

Fully expecting Mitch to need his concentration before the game, Jenny didn't know how to react when Mitch took a moment as he crossed to his side of the court to blow her a kiss.

"Way to go," Bonnie drawled to her as female groans sounded around the stands.

Jenny didn't reply. She was too happy to speak. She didn't have much to say afterward, either, since within minutes her heart was lodged in her throat as she watched Mitch surprise her with how good he was.

The two men probably could have played a polite game and still entertained the female members of the audience. With his dark and compelling presence, Bruce Paxton created an interesting contrast to Mitch's golden-boy persona. But as was often the case, looks could be deceiving. Both men also exhibited a wicked sense of humor, balanced by a definite love for competition. By the third game, with the score one to one, Jenny knew they were intent on playing as if they were the only two in the tournament.

Volley after volley ripped across the net. Mitch would charge to return and win an impossible point, and with the next serve Paxton would do something equally talented.

"This is awful. They're both so good!" Jenny moaned, grateful to have Mary to rock to burn off at least a little anxiety.

Bonnie laughed. "You can say that again. But I think our Mitch has an edge. He's really inspired today."

That seemed true. He won the first set, although not without difficulty. During the brief break, he retired to the sideline where he mopped his face with a clean towel and gulped down some refreshment handed to him by a ponytailed teenager. He should have used the time to sit down and rest; instead, he again looked toward the box and winked at her.

"See what I mean," Bonnie said, clapping her approval.

Indeed. But when the second set began with less promise, Jenny realized how dangerous it would be to take anything for granted.

Mitch stumbled and lost a crucial early point, then went on to lose the game. Looking thoroughly disgusted with himself, he hunkered low as Paxton took to his baseline to prepare to serve.

The second set took twice as long as the first, with Paxton winning. By the third set, Mitch was winning, but tiring fast. Each point came hard-won, and several times he lost ground. When the crucial point came where he could win the match, Jenny thought her dress had to be soaked through and through from built-up tension. The heat from her body had even made poor little Mary's fine blond curls damp. As for the players, as breathless and hot as both looked, they were grinning at each other, but determined not to yield an inch.

Jenny almost missed the end of the match by merely running the back of her hand across her brow. Just in time she saw Mitch deliver a killer serve that must have only cleared the net by a hair. Paxton slammed it back with equal force. Mitch had already begun to move in and shot a return toward the opposite side of the court.

Despite a valiant effort, Paxton couldn't reach it in time.

The crowd leapt to its feet as if witnessing a Wimbledon victory. Bonnie hugged Jenny's neck before jumping up to cheer like the rest. Jenny simply sat there, too exhausted to move, and too overwhelmed by emotion to do anything but feel tears of pride slip down her face.

It was that expression that Mitch saw after he shook hands with Paxton and turned to wave up at her. She saw his grin fade. No, not fade, exactly, but change. And then she lost sight of him completely in the wall of people moving between them. By the time she found a break to peek through, the new competitors were taking the court and Mitch was nowhere to be seen.

He couldn't get to her fast enough. Of all times to suddenly realize you could do without ceremony and attention... Mitch barely made it through the presentation of the trophy and the check to the honored charity in the name of Gulf-West. As soon as possible, he ducked the media and the groupies, took the fastest shower in the history of Texas, slipped into the change of clothes he'd brought along, and raced around the back walkways to get to the Gulf-West box.

He almost tipped Jenny over at the last turn.

"Whoa—Jen!" He took in her tear-stained face, the way she was overburdened with the baby, the bags and things, and quickly grabbed the tote and her shoulder bag from her. "Are you okay?"

"Of course I'm okay. You—"

"Did something happen?"

"No, I—"

"If someone said something... I know the group I work with can be a rowdy bunch, but if anyone said anything, was rude to you—"

"Mitch, would you shut up! Please!"

He reared back. "Jen?"

Her expression softened. "You won."

"Yeah..." He watched fresh tears fill her eyes. So he hadn't been wrong about seeing them before. "So why are you crying?"

"It was wonderful. *You* were wonderful."

"Thanks, but then, shouldn't you be happy?"

"I am happy. And sad. For you, McCord, don't you get it?"

He was afraid not. "I guess I'm missing a technicality or two."

"You're *good*. Better than good. You should have been the pro you dreamed of being, but your heart got broken."

"Don't do that."

He didn't want her to say more. Not here.

Taking hold of her arm, he led her toward the nearest exit. Tomorrow he would deal with a good bit of ribbing from the VIPs who liked to get their money's worth, but this was more important.

Fortunately, most people were staying to watch the doubles matches, so Mitch and Jenny didn't have to detour much to avoid unwanted attention. Despite the shade tree he'd found to park beneath, the car was baking hot. It took Mitch a minute to key the engine and turn the air conditioner on full-force, and then another minute until it was cool enough for Jenny to set the baby in her seat and get in herself.

When she began to set her seat belt, he stopped her. "Now tell me."

She sighed. "I already did. And I'm sorry you were embarrassed because of how I reacted."

"Who said anything about being embarrassed?" Her face was flushed and her hair was damp, but she looked very dear to him. "You cried for me."

"Why do you keep saying that, McCord? Hasn't anyone ever spilled tears over you before?"

"I don't think so. There've been a few women who cried *because* I was a bum, ending a relationship before things got sticky, but... no. This is a first."

"Well, enjoy it," she muttered, blinking hard as she searched in her purse for a tissue. "It's not something I want to do often."

Mitch pulled her back to him and framed her face. "I've never been more touched."

"You're just saying that because you don't want me to feel bad for you, but— My gosh, McCord, to think what your family cost you due to their petty differences and selfish squabbling."

"They didn't cost me anything. I did it. *Me.*"

"They should have supported you. Seen what a talent you have."

"Talent's not enough. I didn't have the drive, the need, the staying power."

"Because you were emotionally stunted—or shortchanged. I don't know what the technical term is—" she said with an exasperated wave of her hand. "But I recognize the tragedy when I see it."

As much as he enjoyed this outpouring of concern and compassion, Mitch couldn't let her continue. He shifted a thumb over her lips. "I made my choices. It's done."

"Oh, Mitch—"

"Why don't you just say congratulations and kiss me."

She got it out of sequence. First she wrapped her arms around his neck and pressed her lips to his. The instant he felt their silky heat, Mitch parted them to slake the thirst that no amount of liquid quencher had been able to satisfy.

This wasn't anything like the sweet, exploring kisses he'd been coaxing from her throughout the week when he'd come home late because he'd been practicing for the tournament. He delved deep into her mouth and stroked his tongue against her, letting her know exactly what she made him feel, and how slow and thoroughly he wanted to love her.

With a sigh, Jenny shifted to slide her fingers into his shower-damp hair. Encouraged, Mitch shifted and pulled her tighter against his chest. Already, despite the refreshing air blowing from the vents, the knit shirt he'd changed into felt like a heating pad. When he felt Jenny's full, firm breasts against him, he thought it a wonder the material didn't melt like nylon on a hot iron.

Angling his head the other way, he intensified the kiss, explored the silky length of her glorious hair, the sleek shape of her back. All the while he plumbed her mouth for more of her essence.

"Congratulations," she murmured when he freed her mouth, only to explore the creaminess of her graceful neck.

"I like your kind of applause. You're not sad anymore?"

"It's difficult to stay that way when you appear so—well—adjusted."

He laughed softly, enjoying her gentle teasing. The sound was echoed by a more delicate one behind them.

Mitch glanced to the back seat and saw that Mary was smiling at him. "Look, she approves."

Jenny did shift around to give a gentle shake to the baby's tiny lacy-socked foot. "You should be exhausted from all the attention you had this afternoon, young lady. Why aren't you sleeping?"

"She must take after her old man." Mitch studied the alluring movement of Jenny's breasts as she faced him again. "Once the adrenaline starts flowing, it's hard to burn it all up."

"Are you trying to tell me something?" she asked, reaching up to stroke his mustache.

"Only that I want your sweet mouth again, Jen. Don't ask me to drive all the way home after just one taste of you."

This time he folded her into his arms from the onset, combed his fingers into the heavy waves of her hair and cupped her head to hold her still while he attempted to sate just a little more of his growing hunger for her. He drank her soft moan, and coaxed her into a sexy tango of tongue against tongue, until he uttered his own throaty satisfaction as her fingers moved restlessly across his shoulders . . . her short nails bit into the muscles along his neck.

He relished the feel of her heart beating against his, her nipples tightening. It was too much to resist and, keeping his head enough to remember discretion, it was his right hand he slid to her waist and then up her side. When he found her breast, he explored the feminine swell first with his thumb. Rewarded with a subtle trembling from Jenny, followed by a less subtle thrust closer, he claimed her with his entire hand.

"Mitch."

"Ah, Jen . . . I've been aching to do this."

"It feels so good."

"I wish we were back at the house. I could make you feel even better. Do you ever think about it? My hands learning the secrets of your body?"

"Almost always...and quite a bit more lately."

"It's been the same for me."

"The truth?"

"Cross my heart."

"Aren't you the guy who told me you couldn't make it as a Boy Scout?"

"Before it was easier to resist you, because I could try to forget in the arms of another woman. But...you have to know that's not the way it is now, Jen."

"Because your life's more complicated."

"It's *not* just the baby," he whispered hotly into her ear. At the same time he stroked his thumb over her again. "You're making hamburger out of all my stubborn theories and wine out of my bitter memories, sweetheart."

She framed his face with her hands and searched deep into his eyes. "That's the loveliest thing anyone's ever said to me. I wish I could believe you."

"I wouldn't lie to you."

"But you could believe you meant something and realize it was a mistake later."

With a muttered oath, Mitch hugged her so tightly to him she had to arch her head way back to keep looking at him. "I'm not some kid who can't control what's in his pants, and I sure as hell don't want a one-night stand with you. In fact, I don't want to rush anything at all. But I do think we are ready to take this relationship onward. I think we're going to find we're damn good together, but I promise you, we won't go any farther than what you're ready for."

To convince her, he took her mouth again, nibbling at her lips, biting gently, before intensifying it to the sensual dance they were learning fast and too well. His body burned like an overworked furnace already. He almost shook at the thought of how it would feel to lower Jenny to his living room couch, peel the straps of her dress off her shoulders and expose her flawless skin for his eyes and his touch.

"Say yes."

Jenny didn't answer, but she didn't stop him, either. And when he initiated the next kiss, she became a whole participant. Someone else with a halo around his head might have been able to resist her, but the one presented to him didn't fit.

He wanted her. He didn't want to scare her off by telling her how much, but he intended that she know. It was in him to wait, to woo her, especially since he couldn't believe this was happening himself. But he couldn't keep his hands to himself totally.

At the very moment he was about to ask her again, he heard a knock behind him. "What the—"

He spun around and saw a man crouched down to peer in the window. It was the last face he wanted to see that afternoon.

Chapter Seven

"Mitch?" Jenny could barely hold back a gasp. "Who's that?"

He didn't reply, not at first, and she was left to wonder if the man staring in the window at them was a panhandler, someone with car trouble, or... He didn't exactly look destitute enough to be a panhandler, but then again, she'd been approached several times in North Dallas by individuals with more jewelry than she owned, aggressively asking for bus fare back to wherever they claimed to be from.

"I'll be right back."

She wasn't sure she heard him right until he reached for the door handle. "Wait a minute," she began in a panic. "You don't even know the man! In this day and age you can never be too careful."

"Yeah, I do."

He did? She could only stare. This wasn't anyone

she'd met in the Gulf-West box. As Mitch climbed out of the idling sedan, Jenny sat too shocked to say more.

The stranger was middle-aged, and of average height and build—except for a bulging belly that suggested he was either six months pregnant or had an affection for beer or sweets. He tried to hide it by wearing his plaid cotton shirt untucked, but the boxy cut and the defined squares of the pink-and-green shirt over white pants only made matters worse. Wild eyebrows over hawklike eyes gave him a slightly satanic look, and his face was pale, flushed and bulb-shiny from his knobby chin to his balding head.

Where on earth had Mitch met a man like this? Jenny hoped he wouldn't close the car door, so she could hear enough to explain. But not only did Mitch shut the door, after shaking the man's hand, he led him several feet away from the car, to stand underneath the shade of the maple tree.

The man spoke fast and gestured back toward the country club, then pulled a handkerchief from a back pocket and dabbed at his face and the top of his head. Mitch's expression began to grow grimmer as the man began to speak faster. Whatever the man was complaining about, it didn't seem to impress Mitch, and he placed his hands on his hips, adding a look that she'd seen when he was about to dig his heels in over something.

Suddenly the man shook his head adamantly and reached into his other back pocket and brought out a folded manila envelope. He handed it over to Mitch, who didn't look happy at all to be receiving it. Expecting him to open it, Jenny witnessed yet another response as he crushed it in his hand.

What on earth...

Mitch snapped at the man, poked him in the chest with his index finger, and walked away from him. Behind him the older man shrugged and hurried away.

Jenny stared as Mitch climbed back into the car. She gnawed a bit at her lower lip when he threw the envelope onto the dashboard and secured his seat belt.

"Fasten yours," he said without looking at her.

"What happened? Who was that?" she asked instead.

"We're leaving, Jen. Fasten your belt, or do you not care if I get a ticket?"

He hadn't exactly been rude, but there was a sharp edge to his voice that told her it would be a mistake to make a flippant reply right now. Deciding to say nothing at all, she shifted over to her side of the car and did as he commanded.

After several seconds he sighed. "I'm sorry. It was wrong to snap at you."

"Do you want to talk about it?"

He shook his head. "No. But I suppose you have a right to know." Backing out of the space, he directed the car toward the north exit. "That was the private detective I'd hired to look for Savannah."

Jenny quietly studied his sharp profile. Gone was the confident, positive man who'd only minutes ago played and won an inspired tennis match. Gone was the tender man who'd held her and touched her as if she were precious to him. Even with the help of the sinking sun that cast an amber, softening hue to everything around them, she couldn't help notice the muscle working in his right cheek.

She wanted to ask what had happened, but thought she might ease him into that by focusing on the man's unexpected presence. "How did he know you would be here today?"

"I left a message on my machine just in case he called. He decided to save himself a drive to New Hope and came out here to find me."

"He certainly seemed anxious to talk to you."

"Yeah," Mitch muttered with disgust. "Anxious to tell me that he was quitting and to present me with his bill."

The guy hadn't looked like a quitter to her. She might not think much of his sense of style, but his eyes and chin had suggested a tenacious personality. "I'm sorry to hear that, but surely he gave you a good reason."

"I don't know how good it was. He got spooked."

Of all the things she expected him to say, it wasn't that. "My goodness...when? Where? How?"

"By getting too close to succeeding, I guess."

"He found her!"

"He thinks he must have because he says someone appeared at his motel in California and warned him off."

"What do you mean, warned him off? Warned as in threatened his *life?*" Jenny didn't intend for the last word to crack in her throat, but she supposed her nerves were getting a bit frayed, too.

"He thinks so."

"But he doesn't know for sure?"

"He was told to stop sticking his nose where it didn't belong, unless he wanted to spend a considerable amount of time and money on plastic surgery. I would say that qualifies as a threat."

"But why would Savannah do that?"

"Hey. I've just heard about this myself. I haven't had a chance to take it in, let alone analyze it!"

Jenny ignored the curt edge that had returned to his voice. This was too incredible a situation to worry about getting her feelings singed. "Your private investigator said more than what you're telling me, McCord. I saw him carrying on at Indy 500 speed!"

"Yeah, he said more," Mitch replied, practically growling the words. "He described the guy as a big moose who looked as if he meant what he'd said. Okay? Happy now?"

Intrigued was more like it. And furious. "What on earth is Savannah up to?"

"I don't know, but I'm going to find out."

They were on 635 again and about to turn north onto Central Expressway. As Mitch concentrated on passing a slower car, Jenny studied the gold fire in his amber eyes. It had nothing to do with the sunset.

"You can't be serious?"

"Never more so."

Jenny took a deep breath, striving to keep the exasperation out of her voice. The crazy man just didn't get it. "It would seem you have your answer, McCord. The lady—and I use the term loosely—appears to know exactly why that detective was looking for her, and she's letting you know that not only is she definitely Mary's mother, but she also doesn't want her back! Why can't you accept that and let things be?"

"Because it's not good enough. She owes me answers . . . an apology. Mary's *birth certificate!*"

"You can go to court and get that."

"I told you before, I'm not going to let the gossipmongers turn Mary's life story into a three-ring circus. She'll have enough to cope with when she gets old enough to go to school and some kid repeats what

Mommy or Daddy were talking about around the dinner table."

Jenny reached over and laid a hand on his arm. "By then she'll be full of confidence from the love you've enveloped her in, Mitch. And maybe you're blowing this out of proportion. New Hope is growing and changing all the time. By then there may be far more scandalous things going on in town. Why, have you noticed Faith Harper at the Baby Boutique is pregnant? I didn't know she was seeing anyone!"

"My mind's made up, Jen."

His answer hurt. Maybe he had a right to do whatever he felt best for his child, but she spent almost as much time with the baby as he did. What's more, hadn't he asked her to return to his house a short time ago? That didn't mean she'd agreed to sleep with him, but they both knew something deeper was developing between them. Didn't that give her some right to an opinion, too?

She couldn't ask, suddenly afraid of what his answer might be. As a result, the rest of the drive back to New Hope felt like a trip to a funeral, not a victory celebration or a romantic prelude.

When Mitch pulled into his driveway and killed the engine, Jenny glanced into the back seat. "She's asleep. I'll carry her up to bed, so you can get her things."

Mitch nodded. Without a word, he collected his bag, the baby's tote and Jenny's purse. Jenny didn't stop to see if he followed, but went straight up to put the baby into the crib Mitch had set up in his former office. Mary roused slightly as Jenny set her down on the cool Mother Goose sheets, and Jenny stayed and hummed a lullaby that she remembered her mother singing to her when she was a child.

Mary's Cupid's bow mouth curved into the sweetest of smiles, although her eyes remained closed. Jenny took in her dusky-blond lashes curling over pink cherubic cheeks and felt her heartstrings being tied into complicated knots.

What a little darling. Jenny wanted desperately to be the one to teach her to say "Da-da," to help her until she could take her first steps alone on those adorable dimple-kneed legs, to teach her nursery rhymes and lullabies that someday she could teach her baby. Why couldn't Mitch see that he was risking all that?

Blinking back a sudden wetness in her eyes, Jenny tenderly kissed the baby's wispy curls and tiptoed out of the room. The hallway was quiet. She had hoped that maybe Mitch had followed her up, but she could hear him moving around downstairs. With a mirthless smile, she went to find him.

Old ghosts. Mitch shut the refrigerator door on the beer he wanted so badly he could feel its cool bite in his belly. But he would be flying again tomorrow, and he religiously lived up to the airline's rule about alcohol. Which meant he would have to take on Jenny cold turkey. Why did he know this was going to feel as if cutting off his own hand might be a simpler thing?

"I think she may stay asleep until your normal waking time in the morning," Jenny said, coming into the kitchen. She went straight for the tote and began unpacking it.

"I can do that later."

"I don't mind."

"But you must be beat, too."

That stilled her movements. "Do you want me to leave?"

He hesitated ... almost too long. As she reached for her purse, he lurched forward and stayed her hand. "No!" Touching her made it easier to find words for things he'd never expressed, let alone felt. "No. But...I don't know how to do this."

"What?"

Her voice was thin, almost fearful. Her eyes held similar emotions, but she kept her chin high. He hated seeing the uncertainty, especially when it was too easy to remember what those eyes looked like when he touched her. But he had always been able to make women want him.

"Do what?" she whispered with more strength.

"Tell you how I feel."

"I thought that's what you were doing while reading me the junior riot act on the way home."

"No. I was reacting and acting, and you know it. Surface stuff, when what you wanted ... You're relentless, Jen. You insist I feel every pore, every cell, if I'm going to be around you."

"Is that so bad?"

"How do I make you understand that I ... I can't do something, be somebody, just because you want that?"

"It's not about what *I* want. You've kept me at arm's length for years, McCord, so don't you dare tell me this is about me. Whatever you're dealing with, it's between you and you. And the way I see it, I think you're fed up with the old way of playing the game. You *do* want to stop kidding yourself, to stop thinking that it doesn't matter if you grow old alone. You *are* concerned about letting opportunity slip through your fingers, but you don't do enough about it because risk doesn't come with guarantees."

"Because I don't want to hurt you."

She dropped her head back and uttered a single, deliberate "Ha!" at the ceiling. "You've been hurting me for as long as I've had this stupid weakness for you. So what else is new? You know what? It's probably time I smartened up."

She did snatch up her purse then. Mitch thought she was impressively agile to get as close to the door as she did before he tugged her back by the strap of her purse. It went flying as he swung her around to face him.

Since the world made more sense when they weren't speaking, he kissed her, swept her into his arms and continued kissing her as he carried her to the living room. It was a miracle he didn't break both their necks, since he moved by instinct and memory alone. Finally, he settled on the couch and held her on his lap.

"Damn you, Mitch. Let me go."

"Have you noticed that it's only when you get unsure of things, or feel vulnerable, that you stop calling me McCord?"

"Yes. And since you have, too, would you please let me go and not take advantage?"

She was shaking, and she didn't want to look at him. Mitch felt an abundance of relief as well as tenderness. Cupping the back of her neck, he coaxed her to submit, to relax against his shoulder. "Sorry, but I can't. I need those weaknesses. They give me the courage to ignore my own."

"You're not making any sense. I think you must be suffering heatstroke from your tennis match."

He made a sound deep in his chest. "The match. Feels like that was a week ago. Or as if it happened to someone else."

"Same here." She tried to free herself again. "I should get home."

"Sit with me a minute, Jen. Let's just finish the day together, feel the sun going down behind us." If they could do that, maybe they could talk about Savannah, Mary, and the future without going combustible.

She didn't agree, but she did stop struggling to get off his lap. When he realized what that meant, he planted a kiss on her forehead.

The glow of amber light poured through the windows behind him and filled the room, warmed it, despite the air-conditioning. Mitch watched it turn a painting of West Texas on the opposite wall into a scene where he could almost taste dust on his tongue and feel grit against his shirt collar and neck. He had flown over that land countless times. Years ago, when he'd done his first solo for his single-engine license, he'd landed out there and felt an odd kinship with the aridity and barrenness. In a way it had been as if he'd been meeting himself.

How could you admire something and still not like it much? he wondered. He wanted to explain that to Jenny, but the words...

He ran his hand from her hair to her hip. "You're a pretty woman, Jenny Stevens...and the first real female friend I've ever had."

"Coward. I'm your *best* friend, McCord."

"True, and a little scary," he murmured with a sigh.

"Don't worry, I'll keep it our secret, in case you blow it eventually. At least that will assure you of one less thing you'll be haunted by."

As she spoke, her breath tickled his neck. He shifted to touch his cheek to hers. "I don't want to blow it. Losing you..."

"You can't if you stop trying to push me away."

"So much for subtle hints."

"I prefer being direct. You and I can't afford—" as he caressed her again, she sucked in a quick, little breath "—misunderstandings at this stage."

Probably. But if he had to be direct, he preferred to choose in what sequence they discussed the topics. Right now all he wanted was to have her mouth again, and he claimed it with the accuracy of one who'd been practicing in his fantasies for a long time.

He liked having her this way, curled against him, trusting. Able to feel almost every inch of each other. Each touch, the subtlest caress, elicited wave after warm wave of intoxicating pleasure. He could only imagine what sweet insanity they could bring to each other if they did become lovers.

"Ah, Jen . . . Jenny. What's going to happen to us?"

"That's your problem, you're trying to have an answer for everything," she said, leaning back to meet his pensive gaze. "You think every day, month, year needs to be planned out, and when you realize that's impossible, you panic. What's wrong with a little spontaneity?"

"In theory, nothing. But the last time I put theory into practice, Mary was conceived," he reminded her drolly.

"You see?" She sat up like a spring toy. "You can't even avoid talking about Savannah. How do you expect me to?"

He sighed. "I suppose I can't."

"Why do you suppose she doesn't want to be found?"

"I don't know. Savannah has traveled in some unusual circles, but to send a thug out to discourage any contact with her . . ."

"Call me crazy, but are you sure she's not involved with some underworld figure?"

"I'm not sure about anything, except that I have to find out what's going on so that it doesn't end up hurting Mary now or later. But you were right before—at least this does indicate she's Mary's mother."

"And that you're her father," Jenny added with a smile.

"Yeah." The word barely made it past the lump in his throat. He had been trying to remain calm about that, especially considering his earlier attitude toward the idea of fatherhood; however, his relief and euphoria told him just how hard he'd been protecting himself the past week. His doubt had quickly turned into a fear that this could be some cruel hoax and that Mary might not be his. What a humbling and heady discovery to learn that was behind him.

"Have you looked inside the envelope that detective gave you?"

Mitch shook his head. "Not yet. This is a shock coming on the heels of a full day. I wanted some time to get used to what it all meant... and to deal with the possibility of having to lose you."

"I told you, you can't do that unless you're doing the pushing. I'm here because I want to be, McCord."

Here came the hard part. He took her hand and studied the slender fingers with their short, impeccable nails. He stroked his fingers over her knuckles. "But when I asked you for help with the baby, I promised that it was temporary. Jen, you're an entrepreneur with schedules and responsibility. I have no right to use the chemistry that's between us to coerce you into jeopardizing all that you've worked for."

Jenny tugged her hand free from his, only to frame his face, leaning close so that they were almost nose to nose. "Now hear this, McCord. It was your decision to come to me. It was mine to help you. If you no longer want my help, all you have to do is tell me. If I don't feel I can give Mary all she needs, plus continue with my business commitments, I'm not going to play martyr. I'll tell you."

"But then there's the personal angle in all this."

Her dark eyes lighting with humor, Jenny lowered herself onto his chest. "That's what really has you nervous. You're afraid that my helping you obligates you somehow. Exactly which of my senses do you believe to be defective? No, I'm fully aware I'm in a situation with a man who is allergic to the word *relationship* ... and horror of horrors, he's also my next-door neighbor. But guess what? It happened."

"Don't think for a second I'm not happy it has," Mitch said, pulling her back up so he could reach her mouth. He kissed her tenderly. "I just need you to know, though, that I still have to do what I feel is right."

"Savannah?"

"Yeah." He watched her shield her eyes by lowering her lashes, understood the vulnerability and doubt that shadowed her face. "You're wrong, you know."

"Am I?"

Mitch knew of only one way to prove to Jenny that he wanted her and no one else. He lowered her to the seat cushion and kept her there with the weight of his body. "Savannah was a mistake. I never think of her."

"Don't say—"

"Correction. I don't think of her except to want to shake her until her capped teeth fall out for doing what she's done." He took in Jenny's lovely but bewildered face, the way her breasts rose and fell from having been caught off guard. "You're the one I think about, Jen. I can tell you things about you, about when you were a kid, that I'll bet you would never guess I remember."

"Like what?"

"That your first grown-up bathing suit was an orange two-piece that made me want to rip off the drapes I was hiding behind and run out to cover you."

Her mouth fell open. "You're kidding!"

"Well, actually, what I really wanted to do would have put me in jail."

"I wish I'd known," she said, reaching up to stroke his chest. "What else?"

"Never mind. I can see I'm going to have to dole out the information sparingly, or else you're going to get a swollen head."

"Little ol' *me?*" Her eyes twinkling, she wrapped her arms around his neck and pulled him downward. "I suppose I could always extract the information in my own way."

"And what way is that?" Mitch murmured, already angling his head to cover her mouth with his.

She didn't answer—but then, she didn't have to, because she was showing him.

How quickly the heart could catch fire. As Mitch felt her arch toward him, he drove his hands into her hair and felt a bit more of his self-control slip. Sweet, tempting Jenny had indeed the talent to bring him to his knees if she wanted. But he knew punishment and control weren't on her agenda. No, all she wanted was wonderful, delirious loving. With him.

She made his head spin, and his body ache. Behind his closed eyes, he saw himself reaching for the straps of her dress, the zipper in the back. He wanted to ease it down, to lower the dress so he could adore more of her. All of her. Prompted by the image, he tore his mouth free to race it across her cheek and down her throat. Her shoulders were elegant, her collarbone delicate. But it was the gentle swell of flesh over the bodice of her dress that lured him, and he trailed his mouth over one mound and then the other.

He wanted to have her completely beneath him, to bury his aching body in the heaven that hers offered. Wanted it so much that he made her gasp from the speed with which he sat up and pulled her with him.

"What's wrong?" she managed, grasping his arms to regain her balance.

"You're right. You can turn me into mush. Particularly tonight. So I'm sending you home."

Jenny could barely keep up as he pulled her to the kitchen, snatched her bag, and led her toward the back door. "Mitch! Don't I get a say in this?"

"No." Before he opened the door, he kissed her. Hard. "Not this time. But don't worry, I'm going to let you try again—soon."

"Maybe I should get that in writing."

With her hair in sexy disarray and her skin glowing, she played pure havoc with his good intentions. One more kiss, Mitch decided, hauling her close. He locked his mouth to hers and let desire rule.

As expected, it flared fast and hot. Far before he sated even the first layer of his need for her, he forced himself to put her at arm's length.

"You don't need anything in writing," he rasped.

Touching his finger to her kiss-swollen lips, he whispered good-night to her and opened the door.

"See you in the morning."

"Count on it."

It hurt like hell to let her go, but he was also proud of himself. There had been a time...

No, the old days were over. He was building toward a future. One step at a time, the way Jenny had suggested. Today had been a good start...not perfect...a bit bumpy here and there, but a start. Tomorrow would be better.

"If you live through the night," he told himself.

Sucking in a deep breath and exhaling the ache Jenny had triggered in him, Mitch stripped off his shirt and headed upstairs. He wanted another shower, a cooler one, and then he planned to check out the envelope J. D. Rogers had given him.

The thing was thick for a statement. Hopefully it contained a full report of all the people the detective had spoken to, as well as all the places he'd searched. Maybe Rogers had been scared away, but the detective didn't have as much to lose as Mitch felt *he* did.

On his way to his room, Mitch detoured to check on the baby. Jenny had complained that the room remained rather barren for her tastes, but she'd succeeded in getting him to move his office down the hall and convert this into a nursery. The crib was the one she had offered, the rocking chair came from her, too. It had been her mother's. She'd said that she heard it would come in handy when the baby began teething and was up and cranky at all hours of the night. At the time he hadn't wanted to let himself believe he would be allowed to be there for his child at those times. Now he was beginning to think there was a possibility it might come true.

Savannah wanted no part of her child. As incredible as the idea seemed to Mitch, she couldn't have given him more welcome news.

"But *I* want you," he whispered to Mary as he bent over her.

Sweet Lord, she was precious. Still dressed in the soft, pink cotton gown and socks from earlier, she lay in the semidarkness with her arms raised over her head and her tiny hands fisted. Mitch grinned, thinking she looked like a miniature Rocky lying in that position.

He knew he should leave her to sleep in peace, but he had the strongest craving to hold her for a few moments. Slinging his shirt over the foot of the crib, he slowly lifted her and settled her in the nest he made with his left arm. This had been quite traumatic the first few times, but it was getting easier with practice; however, her size continued to awe him.

Easing down onto the rocker, he watched her stretch, lift one socked foot and rest it against his chest. Feeling yet another lump growing in his throat, he took hold of that tiny foot and bent to kiss it before setting it on his forearm, in a way he knew would be more comfortable to her.

Slowly he began rocking. He was new at this, too. Mary didn't seem to mind, though. It appeared that babies had a capacity for great patience with beginners. He hoped so because he was going to need a great deal from her.

Emotion built in him. Maybe it was leftover adrenaline. Maybe it was the new ground he'd covered with Jenny and the brightening promise the future held. Whatever the reason, he felt an unexpected wetness around his eyes, so he closed them, and rocked, building another memory he knew he would cherish for the rest of his life.

Chapter Eight

"I think I'm beginning to see less and less of Savannah in Mary every day," Jenny said to her grandmother as she settled Mary in the portable carrier on the kitchen table. She planned to keep the baby near while she typed up a new batch of invoices on her notebook computer.

Having just hung up the phone, her grandmother carried a notepad and cup of tea to join them. "That's because your rose-colored glasses are turning opaque." She sighed as she settled her plump body onto the chair across from Jenny's.

"I don't think so. Mitch has had her for over two weeks now. Babies change quite a bit in the first few months."

Her grandmother adjusted her bifocals and studied her pad. "Hmm... all the hat-and-bootie sets are gone at the boutique, and Agnes told me there's been a run on those white baby blankets with the satin trim, too. I wonder why Faith didn't call me to tell me that herself."

"Gee, could it be because you've been gabbing with Agnes for the better part of an hour?" Jenny drawled. Under normal circumstances she didn't care how long her grandmother talked, but this wasn't just about the phone. It bothered her that her grandmother pretended she hadn't noticed any change in the baby. "Didn't you hear a beep during all that time?"

"Yes."

"Well, that was an incoming call! I've told you how to operate the phone to pick it up." Jenny was glad she'd insisted on getting a second line for her business.

"So I forgot. I am getting on in years, you know."

Jenny turned to the baby. "Did you hear that? This is what's called evasive behavior. You'll notice it when you want an extra chocolate-chip cookie before dinner and she doesn't want to be the bad guy and say, 'No, you'll ruin your appetite.' But in the blink of an eye she can tell you exactly what knit items she's sold this week and what's still out on consignment—down to the color!"

"Of course I remember colors," her grandmother declared with a sniff. "Color is crucial in my business. Take for instance those blankets I was telling you about. They're being grabbed up by people needing christening gifts." She leaned closer to Jenny. "And if you ask me, if this baby epidemic continues, the churches are going to have to have twenty-four-hour service. That reminds me, do you know what Agnes told me? She saw Edwin Fishburn at the sperm bank yesterday! Little Eddie who used to chase you up and down the street on that bike with the training wheels trying to get you to kiss him. Agnes said she didn't know what he could possibly want in there now that his fiancée broke off their engagement.''

"Agnes—Agnes—Agnes! Does that bloodhound post herself at the front door of the place?'' Jenny shook her head, deciding she had enough on her plate without getting involved with what everyone else in town was up to. All she wanted was for her grandmother to stick to one subject, too! "Come on, Gran, tell me the truth. Don't you think Mary looks just like her daddy?''

"All babies are adorable. Instead of focusing on that, what you should be concerning yourself with is, does she have her mother's morals and Friendly Skies's silver tongue? Now there's a genetical conversation piece.''

Although she had once chuckled at her grandmother's old nickname for Mitch—a result of her sometimes being frustrated with him herself—Jenny no longer felt it appropriate. "Can't you call him by his given name?''

"Yes, and I can bend down and touch my toes, too, but what fun is that?''

"The point is that he's changing.''

To her credit, her grandmother did grimace. "I guess. Or so it would seem. On the other hand, a few weeks isn't a guarantee. Look at your Valerie.''

The mention of her friend had Jenny gazing at the laptop's screen but seeing Valerie as she'd looked at the supermarket on Tuesday. "I don't know what to do where Val is concerned. She won't open up. She makes excuses that she's been busy, that she's late for an appointment. She doesn't return my calls. Gran, I'm afraid she and Lucas may be headed for divorce court.''

"They're in the right town for it. Babies and divorce seem to be the only two things going on in New Hope these days."

"At least you're profiting from one of those."

"I can knit only so many booties. It would be nice to try something else for a change, broaden my horizons."

"Have patience. It won't be long before those bootie wearers need toddler sweaters, young miss vests and school sweaters."

That won her a reluctant chuckle from her grandmother, who replied, "You're a hopeless romantic."

"I try."

"What if you get your heart broken?"

Jenny smiled wryly, well acquainted with that tactic. "When I first started making jams and things during summer vacations and I asked you if you thought I could sell them, you worried that I'd get my feelings hurt if no one bought them. But they did. When I started Jams By Jenny between community college business classes, you worried that I'd either get ill from doing too much or lose all the insurance money from Mom and Dad. I didn't do that, either. Haven't I proved to be made of tougher stuff—like *you?*"

"Sure, sure. But there's a difference between a little fatigue and a broken heart." When Jenny began to protest, her grandmother raised her hand. "All right. I'll *try* to keep a positive attitude. What do you want me to do, knit him a sweater?"

"As a matter of fact that might be a nice idea for a Christmas present. Something in navy or a hunter green would flatter his blond coloring."

"I'll think about it."

But there was a small smile playing around her grandmother's mouth, which made Jenny reach over and squeeze her hand. "You're a sweetheart."

Jenny had just gone back to working on the invoices when she heard a familiar sound of footsteps. Seconds later Mitch poked his head inside the glass storm door.

"Anybody home?"

As usual, at the sight of him, Jenny's heart sprouted wings and did some fancy aerial maneuvers. He always looked good to her, but she became all weak and jittery when she saw him in his uniform.

"Daddy's home!" she sang to Mary. The baby's eyes widened in recognition and she lifted her fisted hands, her signal that she was ready to be held.

"How was the air up there?" her grandmother asked in lieu of a greeting as Jenny lifted the baby.

"A bit bumpy. That front we're supposed to get sometime tomorrow is really creating some turbulence farther west. How was the knitting today?" he added with a twinkle in his amber eyes.

Her grandmother shot him a sidelong look. "So you were right about lowering the chair. Go play with your baby."

Jenny winked at Mitch. Yesterday her grandmother had complained that the new chair for her knitting machine was a waste of money because it made her back ache. She hadn't let Jenny even look at the thing to see if she could help. But once Mitch arrived, he'd dismissed her blustering and had it adjusted to suit her height within moments.

"She's in rare form today."

"Uh-oh. And here I was going to ask her for a favor. Hello, sunshine," he added, accepting the baby from Jenny.

The transfer brought them in intimate contact and Jenny's gaze inevitably locked with Mitch's. Memory and desire flashed instantly between them and created quite a little scene behind her grandmother's back. In fact, when Mitch bent his head to tenderly kiss the baby, Jenny could have sworn she felt the caress herself!

"What favor?" she asked, her curiosity piqued.

"I should have asked you yesterday, or even the day before, but... you know I'm off now until Monday."

Jenny nodded, telling him with her eyes that she had been waiting for Friday all week. Was he going to suggest they do something with the baby tomorrow or Sunday?

"Well, even though it's short notice, I thought Fiona might baby-sit for Mary this evening while you and I went to Dallas for a night on the town."

An evening out with just the two of them? Yes, that's what his look spoke of. The days, or rather evenings, since the tournament had been pure bliss, watching him with Mary, the long talks they'd shared after they put the baby to bed, and the longer kisses. But this idea of his spoke of pure romance.

"Oh, Mitch, that sounds so... wonderful. But I'm not sure Gran doesn't have other plans."

Her grandmother took off her glasses and set them on the pad. "What plans?"

"The way you were talking with Agnes, I thought maybe you two had more to discuss and would be seeing each other later on. You often get together with her, Ethel and Minny on weekend nights," Jenny said, shrugging.

Her grandmother rose and wagged a finger under her nose. "That doesn't mean it's become the law. What are you, my social director?'' She turned to Mitch. ''If you needed me . . .''

He took hold of her hands. ''Fiona, you don't know how I need you. I know you expend a good deal of time and energy on behalf of my daughter and I never thank you enough. But it's true.''

Fiona flicked a glance at Jenny. ''Didn't I tell you? Sterling silver. So what are you going to wear?''

''She's one of a kind,'' Jenny said once Mitch had the sports car backed out of his driveway. ''Just when I think I have all her moves down pat, she does this to confuse me.''

Mitch grinned. ''Good. Join the club, since that's how I usually feel about you.''

''I'm not that . . . changeable. Am I?''

He shot her a quick but speaking glance. ''What you are is breathtaking.''

What a transformation she'd made from the demure homemaker outfit she'd been wearing when he'd arrived, to the chic black number she had on now. If she tended to wear things that showed her legs to such advantage and her trim figure, he would definitely have given up trying to behave himself a long time ago.

''Thank you,'' she said softly. ''I didn't think you could look more handsome than in your uniform, but . . . wow.''

Delighted by her slightly embarrassed demeanor, he reached for her hand to give it a quick squeeze before he had to shift gears. ''That's one of the things I admire as much as I enjoy about you.''

''What?''

''Your honesty. You say what you mean. Believe me, it's refreshing.''

Jenny looked skeptical. "Come on. You don't get your share of compliments?"

He got looks, most of them the come-hither variety. A different thing entirely. "Let's just say that what *you* say feels real."

She chuckled and relaxed more in her seat. "Well done. If you ever decide to give up flying, I do believe you could have a fine career in the diplomatic service." She indicated his direction. "Where's this motorized magic carpet headed?"

The fact that she didn't take him seriously reminded Mitch that they were still inching through the trust and confidence arena, but the important thing, he told himself, was that they were making progress. "Friday nights tend to be noisy at most restaurants, but there's one in a hotel not far from downtown that has a quieter ambience and a great menu. At least, that's what Neil told me."

"You've never been there before?"

"Um, no." In the past he would have avoided a place where conversation was to be the entertainment of the evening, and he fully expected Jenny to ask him about that. When she didn't, he glanced over at her.

"Does that sound okay?"

"It sounds lovely. Just one question—you don't turn into a pumpkin at midnight, do you?"

"That's definitely not the plan," he murmured. For either of them.

When he'd mentioned the subject of dinner with Jenny to Neil, and asked him to suggest a place where you didn't have to injure your vocal cords or know signing to speak to the person across from you, his friend had given him several of his choice preferences. Neil was known as a husband who got an *F* in dish washing and an *A* in making it up to his wife by taking her out for frequent romantic dinners. As soon as they were seated in the dimly lit restaurant, Mitch decided he owed Neil a good bottle of wine in gratitude.

"This is lovely," Jenny murmured once they were alone.

Mitch took one more look around the room that resembled a formal library before focusing on her. "Not too tweedy and reserved for you?" They did appear to be among the youngest diners there.

"I'm rather fond of tweedy and reserved."

Until they'd walked in here, he hadn't realized that he was, too.

After they ordered, he touched the ivory petal of the rose floating in the carved crystal bowl. "Nope," he murmured.

Jenny's expression turned wounded. "You don't like it? I think it's a perfect touch to offset all the masculinity. And white flowers have always been a special favorite."

"I wondered if it was as soft as your skin. It isn't." He smiled into her eyes. "Why white?"

The blush that crept into her cheeks also made goose bumps rise on her bare arms. "I'd better be careful with the wine. I haven't even had any yet and already I feel as if I've drunk half the bottle."

Mitch stroked her arm, delighted by her sensitivity to his words. "So why white?"

"There seems to be a natural poetry to white flowers. It's at once romantic but melancholy...pure yet mysterious...innocent and exotic."

"You do realize that you've described yourself, don't you?"

As she avoided his intense gaze, her long lashes swept low over her cheeks. "Afraid not. I'm too spirited and feisty. I'm more of a . . . yellow."

He would let her protest all she wanted but his opinion remained firm. "So it's your grandmother who's the pink fan?"

"Isn't it amazing? She pretends to be so gruff and unflappable, but she's a marshmallow at heart. You should see her bedroom."

"Let me guess, it's cotton candy pink?"

"Passionate, powdery, pale or petulant—her room has it all. She's very unprejudiced about her pinks."

Mitch was still chuckling as their wine arrived. Once they were served and alone again, they touched glasses and he murmured, "To tonight."

As they tasted the wine, a pianist in the lounge began playing softly, adding to the soothing, intimate atmosphere. Black-suited waiters passed and Mitch noted their discreet glances toward Jenny. He couldn't blame them. The luster of her hair invited a man's hands, the V-neck cut of her sleeveless dress, though tasteful, drew the eye to the perfection of her skin. He supposed he should be grateful that the tablecloth hid the rest of her, or there might be some traffic accidents. At the same time it amused him that she didn't appear to notice.

He leaned closer until they were elbow to elbow. "So tell me, why the food business?"

"What a question."

"Belated, I know, but humor me. I used to think you were appeasing your grandmother, that she nudged you into it."

"Quite the opposite. She wanted me to use my business degree and go into banking or real estate. It's the look that appealed to her. A woman can be a receptionist or bank teller, some entry position, but if she's in business attire, my grandmother is very impressed."

"And you prefer steamy kitchens and lots of dirty pots and baking dishes?"

"Are you kidding? Why do you think I've gone through two dishwashers since I started this? I chose food because it's—" she gestured discreetly to indicate the other diners in their periphery "—sensual. The colors, the textures, the reaction on the palate. Food has always seemed a combination of art and magic to me, and at the same time nourishing. That's why I designed my own labels with their marbled and Monet watercolor tones. I love to sit down after a batch of preserves is done and turn a jar around and around, put it on a windowsill and watch the play of light coming through."

"I had no idea."

Jenny shrugged. "Maybe no one has figured this out but me, but I keep hoping that my products will make you linger a bit longer at the dinner table with a friend or family member."

"A different kind of stress therapy," Mitch murmured.

"Exactly."

He sighed, thinking back to all those times she'd offered him samples and he'd declined. "Now I feel like a bum for turning you down so often."

"It's just as well," she replied, her eyes lighting with mischief. "Once you taste my product, you'll become addicted."

"That, I already know. Don't forget . . . I *have* kissed you."

It came as no surprise that dinner evolved into exactly the kind of experience Jenny had described. Mitch knew his Caesar salad had never tasted so piquant, his steak more tender, and although he wasn't the world's most enthusiastic sweet eater, he insisted they order at least one dessert to share with their coffee.

When the chocolate torte came with its white chocolate and raspberry sauce, just the thought of getting to feed the delicacy to Jenny, to see her lips part, her tongue peek out to savor every bit of flavor, made him reach for the last swallow of his wine. He knew that all she had to do was see the fork tremble within his fingers and she would know exactly what he wanted to do. Then he met her watchful gaze and knew he'd been set up.

He leaned his elbows on the table and moved his head in closer to her so that they were almost nose to nose. "Wonder who's going to cry 'uncle' first?"

"It doesn't matter, does it? Finding out is what's going to be fun."

It was heaven and hell combined. Their gazes rarely broke, except to close their eyes in ecstasy. Their movements became synchronized, as smooth as a ballet. By the time they'd each had two bites, he could swear he could taste the confection he slipped into her mouth.

"If I don't kiss you soon, I'm going to die," he said at last, his lips barely moving.

"I know exactly how you feel. But the waiting is delicious, too."

Only if you were into torture. In the end, Mitch signaled their waiter and paid the bill. He'd already changed his mind about asking her if she would like to have a nightcap in the lounge and dance. He knew better than to ask for trouble.

As it was, he could hardly wait for the valet to bring their car up front. The driver's door barely shut before he shoved the car into gear and took off.

"Mitch—your seat belt," Jenny said, concern in her voice.

"I know."

If she hadn't been able to tell what he had in mind by the way he gripped her hand as he walked her out of the hotel, he thought the tension in his voice surely gave him away. But when he failed to turn onto the busy street, and instead parked in a dark and solitary part of the lot, he could tell she was surprised.

"Didn't you think I was serious?" he asked, shutting off the engine. Not even waiting to release her from her seat belt, he leaned over in search of her mouth.

He felt his name vibrate on her lips, her hands skim his chest, his cheek. She might as well have been a sparrow fighting to resist collision. But he wanted that impact. Need was a coil inside him, tightening and threatening to shut off oxygen to his brain, blood to his heart.

Finally she sensed that . . . or else she surrendered to her own need. Her hands stilled, her fingers slipped inside his suit jacket, and her lips parted.

He groaned when her tongue met his. She felt like hot, liquid silk, and he felt her heat through every limb in his body. The fleeting memory that once he'd thought her all sugar and untouchable mocked him. Jenny was sweet, yes, but that wasn't all. She was as *whole* a woman and complex as that extravagant dessert they'd just experienced. Now he wanted to experience more of *her*.

The kiss kept changing, from exploring, to ravishing, to savoring. It seemed that no sooner had one

emotion taken hold than another bubbled up from
some deep spring, unending and relentless. Even though
he knew he would be wiser to leave her in her seat, he
found himself fumbling with her seat belt and his seat
levers to slide back and pull her onto his lap.

"I know, sweetheart," he murmured when she whispered his name as if in caution. "I haven't forgotten
where we are." *Entirely.* "But you feel so good."

"You do, too."

"Taste so good."

"Mmm..."

"I need a little more."

With her half lying across him, he kissed her over and
over. As he did, he encouraged her to touch and explore him, just as he intended to add to his frustrat-
ingly limited knowledge of her delectable body. Her silk
dress was sheer provocation and whatever she wore beneath it felt equally fine. The material whispered to him,
much the way she did when he touched her breasts, her
hip, her thigh.

Her restless movements had loosened her neckline.
Mitch took that as a blessing and slipped his hand inside.

"Perfect." He breathed the word against her lips as
he molded and cherished her.

She arched against him. "Let me feel your mouth."

A shudder swept through him. He'd been aching to
do that for so long, and without another moment's
hesitation, he lifted her for that intimate kiss. Jenny's
gasp pierced the sultry silence, her fingers tightened to
an almost painful grip in his hair. But it was the way she
moved, the sensual writhing of her hips against his that
warned Mitch of being too close to risk more.

He tore his mouth from her and pressed her head against his chest to keep her still. "Uncle," he rasped into her hair.

Her breathless laugh sounded as strained as he felt. "You're just being a gentleman. But I adore you for it."

Mitch buried his face deeper into the fragrant mass of silk. "Make no mistake, I want you, Jen. I want to make love to you more than I can remember wanting anything in my life."

"Desire's enough, Mitch. You don't have to—"

He lifted his head and put his thumb over her lips. "Don't. Don't sell yourself short. Whatever you might think, I don't say things just to get my way. You..." He had to hold her close to him again. "You're doing serious things to my head and heart, Jen."

"I know what it cost you to say that, and I wish I could think of something clever and witty to say to take off the pressure. But all I can think is that I'm relieved ... and so glad."

He smoothed back her hair and kissed her temple. "The guy you're talking about was the old Mitch. One of these days, you're going to believe that."

Jenny smiled up at him. "I'm trying."

The longing in her eyes went through him like a laser. "Damn. We should be on that dance floor back there, or I should be taking you to another place," he muttered, disgusted with himself. "The evening, as they say, is relatively young. What's more, I should be repaying you for all you do for me. But all I can think of is peeling you out of that sexy dress, wanting to hear the sounds you make as you come apart in my arms."

"What I do for you and Mary doesn't require repayment. And do you really think we could do a very good job on a dance floor right now, McCord?"

He managed a rueful chuckle. "Not without getting arrested at any rate." He ended the laugh in a deep sigh, willing the ache to ease. "I wish..."

"Don't, Mitch." This time she was the one to pull back. "Whatever you were about to say would be, in a way, regretting Mary. You'll break my heart if you say you do."

"No. *No.*" He took her hand and planted a fervent kiss in her palm. "I'm getting to the point where I believe I was always meant to have her."

"I'm glad." Jenny stroked his cheek. "But then... what's wrong?"

After last week's run-in with that detective and the subsequent disagreement he'd had with Jenny regarding Savannah, Mitch had tried to avoid any mention of what he was doing. The last thing she needed to hear was that he was sending out feelers whenever he flew into Los Angeles. So far there had been a few promises from people who said they would pass on his number *if* they heard from her. He wasn't about to confess as much to Jenny. How he wished he could find a way to resolve this mess without leaving her feeling vulnerable in the process. The problem was, he didn't think Savannah would surface unless he was out there himself making life uncomfortable for her with his inquiries.

Jenny... he was in love with her. He didn't know exactly when it struck him. The first time he'd seen her with Mary? The first time he'd kissed her? All he knew for certain was that this was the woman he wanted to spend the rest of his life with. The woman he wanted as Mary's mother. But could marriage work?

She cared for him, even thought herself in love with him. Unfortunately, he wasn't entirely convinced she knew what love was. Why, she rarely dated, and he would bet every trophy in his house that she was still a virgin! Jenny could be fooling herself, and that left him with the strong fear that part of her emotions were confused with simple decency. That her compassion had gotten muddled up by sexual attraction.

Heaven knows, he knew what he was talking about. He'd seen his parents' marriage wither, decay and die because they let sex lure them into an incompatible relationship, from which none of them ever recovered. That's what people forgot to think about. It wasn't just a matter of one woman and one man. If there were children involved, they suffered, too. He couldn't bear to think of that happening to him, Jenny and Mary. That's why he had to fight this constant battle to keep his desire and his dreams in check, until things were resolved. Until he was certain that he could have a future and Jenny.

"Nothing," he said, kissing her tenderly before setting her back in her seat. "Nothing that won't resolve itself eventually." One way or another, he added to himself.

"Then it's legality worries about Mary. Am I right? You're concerned with how to prove she's legally yours?"

He didn't want to get into that tonight, and he didn't want Jenny worrying about it at all. He knew she didn't want him to have any contact with Savannah, and he grabbed at the easiest way to stop her from talking about it—at least for a while. "Er...no. Well, maybe before, but not now. I've decided to take your advice and go see a lawyer. Brad Tyson told me to do that back when this first happened, but...hell, you know the rest."

"I'm glad you've changed your mind." Even in the dark, relief was evident in her expression. "I'm sure an attorney can get you the results you want."

Perhaps the legal ones, but only Savannah herself could give him critical answers to the questions haunting him. He just hoped he succeeded in getting them before Jenny discovered he wasn't telling her everything—and before his determination to keep his hands off her slipped once too often. It would seem time was becoming crucial in more ways than one.

Chapter Nine

"Are they crazy? It's *crucial* I get back to Dallas to-night!" Mitch snapped at Neil as the two stood outside the gate to the plane.

"Hey, I'm not going to be any hero, either, if I don't get home in time to stay with the kids while Bonnie goes to her friend's wedding shower, but from the looks of things we both have some phone calling to do. The mechanics said the hydraulic problem looks more severe than we initially thought and they want to keep the plane overnight just to be sure they don't miss any-thing."

"I know, I know." This was the second time Neil was explaining this to him, due to *his* poor attitude over the situation. "And the powers that be want us to stay here and wait for the plane instead of taking back a replace-ment." With a heavy sigh, he rubbed the tension build-ing in the back of his neck. When they'd realized all was not well on their approach to LAX, there hadn't been time to acknowledge the stress building up inside them. Their focus had been on getting the plane and everyone in it on the ground and safe. But now with the danger past, Mitch had one humdinger of a headache building at the back of his neck and the base of his skull. "Hell...at least tell me all the passengers have been rerouted onto other flights."

Neil nodded. Despite the fact that he'd been in that cockpit, too, and had a need to get home, he looked amazingly calm and good-natured about the whole thing. "Every last one. That's the good thing about this happening in late September. Vacation season is over, the holiday season hasn't begun, and we were going to have a half-empty plane anyway. Come on, Mitch-o. Cheer up."

"What for?"

With a sardonic look, his first officer drawled, "Think of how much worse things could have been."

Shame cooled Mitch's temper faster than a Blue Norther chilling the Texas landscape. He pinched the bridge of his nose and called himself several varieties of fool. "Sorry for being a jerk. Is there anything else we need to do before we head to the hotel?"

"Everything's been taken care of. I even called over to our favorite hotel to make sure they had a couple of rooms for us." Neil adjusted his hat on his head before slapping Mitch on his back. "Let's get a cab and make the best of a bad situation."

Less than ten minutes later they were in the thick of traffic, watching warily as their cabbie tried to break the sound barrier with a vehicle that appeared to be held together with electrical tape. "This is about right," Mitch said out of the side of his mouth to his fellow passenger. "We averted a crash landing so we could die in a car wreck."

"I was just thinking along those same lines myself. Maybe we should talk about something to keep our minds off Rocket J. Squirrel up there."

"How about the fact that I haven't updated my will yet to take care of Mary?"

Neil winced. "That's not quite the direction I had in mind. What about this evening? Were you and Jenny planning something special?"

"You could say that. It's a month today since Mary was left on my steps."

The dark-haired man's handsome face lit with pleasure, only to crinkle with sympathy. "Ah...blast. No wonder you're upset. What was the plan?"

"Just a little dinner Jen was planning at her place." *The family,* Mitch thought, experiencing a tug of yearning. "Listen, I'm sorry. I shouldn't have gotten bent out of shape the way I did."

"You had every right. Look at it this way, this is as much an anniversary for you and Jen as it is for you and Mary."

That's how he felt. He should have known Neil would understand.

Life was growing so sweet. Almost perfect. He no longer tried to search for excuses to keep some distance with Jenny. Lord, he could barely wait to get home to her and the baby. And despite the fact that she was already beginning to double her production to prepare for holiday order demands, they were able to share many hours together, discovering and cherishing. He resented that he would have to miss even one hour, let alone an entire night.

"So what's the status on you two?" Neil said, breaking into his thoughts. "Bonnie keeps asking me when we're going to get a wedding invitation."

It was due—Mitch knew—and no less than what his heart wanted. But his mind kept putting up road-blocks. For one thing, he'd remained unsuccessful in making contact with Savannah, and despite what he'd said to Jenny, he hadn't sought out an attorney yet. It was getting increasingly tougher to think up an excuse whenever she asked about how things were going there. Lies built on deceit to do things his way—to pacify his doubts. On the other hand, the whole situation *had* only been going on for a matter of weeks.

"We want to make sure everything is right. Rushing into things can create problems later," he told his friend. But he had to wonder if Neil found the words as forced and artificial as he did.

"Right. Let Uncle Neil give you a piece of advice, pal. Waiting for the right moment doesn't mean a dang thing after the kind of flight we had today. You do what you know is right in here." The first officer thumped his chest. "You don't owe anyone any explanations that way."

Mitch was still thinking about the advice when he finally made it up to his room. As a result, the first thing he did after tossing his hat on the bed and stripping off his jacket was to reach for the phone and dial Jenny's number.

"Stevens and Stevens," the familiar, elderly voice intoned. "Senior Stevens here unless you're selling something. And if this is you, Agnes—"

"Fiona . . ." Sometimes, Mitch thought with a wry smile, Jen's grandmother could be worse than a kid. "What are you doing?"

"Mitchell. Is that you? I thought you might be some salesperson. They've been such an annoyance lately. They seem to know just when Jenny's stepped out. Then they all call to sell everything from light bulbs to Limburger. I can no more get to my chair when—"

"Sorry to hear that." He would suggest a cordless phone when he got back. Right now he had other priorities. "Is Jenny there?"

"No, I told you. She left and the phone started ringing."

Mitch massaged his neck again and tried to remember if Jenny had said anything about a scheduled appointment. "Do you know if she'll be back soon?"

"Oh, of course she will. It was just a dash into town to the Baby Boutique to pick up a few things for tonight. Something special for the baby. You know."

He felt that all-too-familiar tightening around his heart. "Yes, tonight." The only way he stopped an expletive for the injustice of it all was to rub his hand over his mouth until he overcame the impulse. "Fiona, tell you what...take down my number, okay? But tell Jenny that I have to step outside for a few minutes myself, and that I'll call her back shortly."

Once he hung up he automatically reached for his jacket. Jenny was out getting something for Mary. He should have thought of that himself. The least he could do was go out to see if he could find a gift downstairs. He and Neil had made arrangements to have dinner together, but he would be back by then. In the meantime—

Mitch opened the door and his mind went blank as he stared at the blonde in leather and sunglasses.

"One month, huh?" Faith Harper massaged her back as she rose from her stool behind the counter and came around toward Jenny. "I don't know that I've heard of anyone celebrating a birthday every month, but that's not to say I don't appreciate the sentiment."

As she approached her, Jenny couldn't help but focus on the maternity blouse Faith wore over jeans. No, what she couldn't help staring at was Faith's swelling belly. Because Jenny had been coming in quite a bit lately—Mitch kept telling her she was going to spoil Mary with all the gifts she was buying, but she couldn't seem to resist the cute things she kept finding—she had been witness to the changes. But she hadn't quite figured out how to ask about Faith's condition without sounding like someone from the FBI. So far, Faith hadn't been any help, either. Usually friendly and fairly up-front about things, these days the lovely shop owner was more tight-lipped than the Raggedy Ann dolls she sold.

"Um, Faith...I can't ignore it anymore." Jenny gestured toward the other woman's stomach. "How far along are you?"

"Almost seven months," Faith replied, placing a protective hand over the gentle swell. Her expression grew tender, though a bit sad, too. "At first I was a bit rattled over the realization that I was pregnant, but now...I can't wait."

She wasn't the only one who'd found it a surprise. Faith had been brought up in a strict home by her aunt. Although her aunt was gone now, nothing in her behavior had ever suggested to Jenny that she was wild or indiscriminate.

"I imagine," Jenny murmured, searching for the right thing to say. She had a million and one questions, but after those few words, Faith went silent again. If the woman didn't want to offer further information, what right did she have to meddle? Jenny thought with an inner sigh. Since she grew weary of gossipers like Agnes and her cohorts, she wasn't about to turn into a younger version herself! "Well! You're certainly in the right business. Do you know who I heard wanted to get pregnant as soon as she can? Michelle Parker. We met the other day at the card shop. She was ordering her stationery for the thank-you notes for after the wedding."

Faith looked away, but her cheeks turned a near peony pink. "I—I don't know Michelle well."

"Oh. I thought I remembered you being at her and Michael Russo's engagement party?"

Faith's smile was forced. "Well, yes, but—" She paused in front of a display of bathtub toys. "Oh! How about something like this? These arrived only yesterday and I've already taken a set myself."

Already forgetting about Michelle and Michael, Jenny picked up the cellophane package. It consisted of a large foam duck, and between the raised wings was a pocket filled with half a dozen yellow-foam baby ducks with orange bills. "Why, they're adorable!"

"The idea of filling the tub with bubble bath and bathing with my baby really appealed to me," Faith continued, her eyes dreamy as she held up a package of her own. "And look, the mother duck's back is made so that it's large enough and sturdy enough to hold the baby if you wanted, or it can be the storage spot for soaps and shampoos and things."

"I'll take it," Jenny replied just as the phone rang. "Oops. Why don't you go get that and I'll browse around a bit more."

With a murmur of thanks, Faith hurried away, leaving Jenny to watch her with admitted curiosity. She supposed she could be exaggerating the other woman's nervous reaction, but— The bell above the door sounded as another customer entered the store, one Jenny was very happy to see.

"Valerie! What a wonderful surprise!"

When her friend spotted her, she waved and, beaming, hurried to her. "What have you got there? Still spoiling your charge?" Valerie asked, giving Jenny an enthusiastic hug.

"What can I say?" Jenny made a face, but quickly added a grin. "*You're* in an awfully good mood. That's nice to see. I've been worrying about you."

"I know," Val replied with a sigh. "And I do appreciate it. But... well, the only way I can think to tell you is just to blurt it out. Lucas and I have received the most bizarre and incredible news. Joe Danson and his wife Carrie were tragically killed in a recent accident. Joe and Luke had been friends since they were kids and now we've just learned that we're the guardians to their two children! Can you believe it?"

No wonder her friend looked both stunned and animated. "My goodness...no, I can't imagine that. In fact I don't know whether to congratulate you or sympathize."

"I know what you mean. When we got the call, Lucas and I could only sit there and stare at each other. But now..." Valerie clasped her hands together. "I can't help but believe that this is a sign for us that we were meant to work out our problems and stay together."

Jenny had only to think of Mitch's background to know that children didn't automatically guarantee that. It wasn't, however, her place to point that out. Instead she focused on trying to understand more of what had happened to her friend. "So there's two children?"

"Two beautiful little girls. I'm here to add to their wardrobe while they're napping with Lucas."

"*Lucas* is napping?"

"It's only been two days and he's exhausted." Valerie's gaze wandered to the front of the store where Faith had put a customer on hold and was checking a display for a certain item. Valerie's eyes went wide and she nudged her elbow into Jenny's side. "Psst...do I see what I think I see?"

"You must have been in another world," Jenny said, shaking her head with concern and sympathy.

"Jen, *you* could be pregnant and I probably wouldn't have noticed it." Valerie nodded toward Faith. "What's the story there?"

"A real mystery...and she's not talking. Reminds me of someone else I know."

Valerie gave her a wry look. "I needed time, Jen. We'll get together soon and I'll fill you in. Besides, you have to meet the girls."

"And you have to see Mitch's Mary."

Her friend tapped her palm against her forehead. "Where's my brain—how *is* that coming along?"

"Wonderful. Terrific."

"You're in love. Why did I bother to ask?"

"Please don't sound as if that's bad news."

"Not bad, more like worrisome. Mitch hasn't let himself be caught yet. He's managed to charm you into providing day care for his baby, and I'm afraid you think now that you're seeing him regularly, it means more than it does."

"It's true." Jenny failed at fully suppressing the stab of pain her friend's words caused. "But we've become very close."

Valerie bit her lower lip, then abruptly hugged Jenny. "I'm sorry. After being an absolute slug of a friend, I have no right to criticize. And I do hope things work out for you two, but... be careful, okay? Protect that tender heart of yours."

By the time Jenny paid for Mary's present and promised to visit Val and her expanded family soon, they were back to chatting with their old enthusiasm. Jenny said goodbye to Faith and Valerie and left the shop with a smile at the bell ringing behind her. But her smile wilted somewhat as she headed for her car. It hurt to think even her dear friend believed Mitch couldn't fall in love with her.

Never mind. Once Mitch gets that paperwork done with his attorney, the path will be free and clear for us to focus on each other, and then everyone will see the Mitchell Sean McCord I know and love.

With a smile for the cellophane package sparkling on the seat beside her, Jenny headed for home.

"Savannah."

She signaled for him to let her enter, and as soon as he stepped back, she rushed inside.

"Don't just stand there. Shut and lock the door!" As soon as Mitch did, she whipped off her sunglasses. "Did you see anyone in the hall? Anyone loitering around that looked suspicious?"

"Besides you? No."

She made a face on her way to the wall-to-wall windows. Standing behind the opened drapes, she parted the sheers to look down on traffic three stories below. "Things seem to be all right, but..."

"Are you rehearsing for a commercial?" Mitch asked drolly. "Something to peddle sunglasses or the latest fragrance?" Heaven knew she reeked of something.

"You think this is funny? You think this is simple? Didn't you get the message I sent through your detective?"

"*You* sent that thug after him?"

"I couldn't very well go myself. How effective would that be? Besides, Bunny is the biggest, roughest-looking character I know. He's been the bouncer at my favorite club since it opened."

Mitch threw his jacket back on the bed and raked his hands through his hair. He had a feeling that this was going to take a while to sort through.

The mother of his child paced to the dresser mirror to inspect her makeup and check her hair. He stared at her as if this were the first time he was seeing her, and in a way it was.

She was as sleek and polished as her white leather pantsuit. Mitch wondered if she'd needed a crowbar to get into the thing, and how many steps were in the process of putting those layers and layers of highlights in her naturally blond hair. It probably took her as long as it did to put on her makeup. He couldn't resent her for wanting to look good—she was in a business where that mattered. But he was beginning to loathe himself for succumbing to the artificialness that was behind her beauty.

She stopped primping and smiled at him in the mirror. "It's good to see you again, Mitch. You're not angry with me, are you?"

"Angry? I'd like to—" He forced himself to take a deep breath, aware that even thinking about violence would serve no purpose and might jeopardize everything. "Just tell me why?" he asked instead.

"Well, you were fifty percent of the process, sugar. I did the hard part—and believe me, it was no picnic—so it came to me that the rest should be your responsibility."

"Just like that?" Mitch put his hands on his hips. "What kind of person are you? No *mother* does that to a child she's given birth to!"

"This one did." Savannah wheeled around, her silver-and-gold mane fanning, her blue eyes snapping. "Listen, Mitch, I could have avoided a pregnancy altogether. And believe me, I knew it would be no simple feat to get this body back into a size six. But I felt obligated to do the right thing."

"The right thing! You turned my life upside down!"

"You're breaking my heart. I lost a bunch of good roles as a result of that pregnancy."

"You had to put her on my steps like that? Without the slightest proof that she *was* my child?"

Savannah's expression turned mocking. "If I knocked on the door and then handed her to you, or signed the note, would you have been willing to keep her?"

"Yes, I would."

"Ha! This is not a good time to pretend being something you're not. Or weren't at the time," she amended, wagging a finger at him. "But I had a hunch about you, and I played it out."

Now she'd piqued his curiosity. Mitch frowned. "What kind of hunch?"

"One that told me that way down deep you're a decent guy." Savannah set the thin shoulder bag in the same white leather on the dresser, and literally draped herself in the armchair beside it. "Why do you think I chose you to take me back to my hotel the night after that ridiculous school reunion last fall?"

He'd assumed because she knew he'd always had a crush on her. He'd hoped that she was finally realizing that she'd had the hots for him. It had been a theory overenhanced with a bit too much beer and wine, and by the next morning he'd acknowledged it as a fantasy that should have been left unfulfilled. Of course, he wasn't about to admit any of that.

"I don't know," he said, not sure he wanted to hear what she had to say.

"You were the closest thing to a knight on a white horse in that place. You were polite, you weren't losing your hair already," she said with a snicker. "You didn't grab me when you asked me to dance, and..."

Mitch saw her expression turn vague, a little sad, as she remembered something. "And?" he asked, prompting her.

"That was a tough time for me. I'd ended a relationship that was headed nowhere and I needed someone to be nice to me. Someone who believed in me the way *I* believed in me. I picked you."

She'd used him. He couldn't believe it. Worse, he didn't realize he'd spoken out loud until she burst into laughter.

"We used each other. So what else is new, particularly in this town."

Mitch recovered from his embarrassment quickly enough, once he realized that she had already moved on and was once again drifting into her own thoughts. "Then you found out you were pregnant," he said, hoping that would get her back on track.

"No, then I met Hugo."

Why hadn't he realized sooner that Savannah had been ditzy? He sat down on the edge of the bed. "Who's Hugo?"

"You've never heard of Hugo Hanover?" When Mitch shook his head, she groaned at the ceiling. "He's only one of the most successful and revered producer-directors in the business, and *not* just in Hollywood, either. I'm talking worldwide. Did you see *The Girl and the Flamingo*? *Rita's Rooster*?"

"Sorry."

"Well, it's not as if they'd be shown in *New Hope*. They're very deep, very metaphorical art films."

"Ah."

"We met at the airport. The heel of my shoe got stuck in a sidewalk crack just in front of his limo. Isn't that incredible?"

"I'm blown away. *Then* you realized you were pregnant?"

She shook her head while admiring a perfect coral fingernail. "Not for a few weeks. You know...when something that's supposed to happen didn't happen?"

That had Mitch starting to feel exceedingly uncomfortable. If the air conditioner wasn't set at near-arctic temperatures, he would have broken out in a sweat beneath his mustache. "Uh, wait a minute. Didn't you say you'd already met Hugo by then? Are you saying you and he didn't..."

"We did. Are you kidding? Mitch, I'm trying to explain—this was sheer *destiny*. But Hugo's enormously disciplined," she added, flipping her hair over her shoulder. "We always practiced safe sex."

Strike two. Mitch massaged the pain that was threatening to crack open the back of his skull. "I see."

"I'll tell you what a great guy he is, when I told him about my condition, he sent me to his beach house in the Carolinas. He paid for the hospital and everything."

Mitch narrowed his eyes, not caring if the guy provided her with a pedicurist every week. "Whose name is listed as the father on the birth certificate?"

"Yours."

It was amazing how quickly the pain began to ease. "And what's Mary's real name?"

"Mary?" Savannah gave him a strange look. "You call her Mary?"

"I had to call her something. I liked Mary. It suited her. It suits the town where she's going to grow up," he added meaningfully.

For the first time a softness stole into Savannah's heavily mascaraed eyes. "I had them put Shawna Mary McCord on the birth certificate. I remembered your middle name was Sean, and Mary seemed a sweet name for a good girl." Her gaze held Mitch's. "I want her to be a good girl, Mitch."

The emotion building in his chest kept him from answering right away. She'd spoken of destiny, and if Mary's name didn't reflect just that, he didn't know what to believe in anymore.

"Thanks," he began, his voice thick. "Um, you didn't want your parents to know about her?"

"They're gone. I have an aunt somewhere in Kansas, but we've never kept in touch. No, she's better off with you. You're glad now that you have her? I was right?"

"She's changed my life."

Savannah began to say something else and then made a negative gesture. "Don't tell me about her. It's better to make a clean break."

"You're back with Hugo? You're okay?"

"Better than okay. We're getting married next week. He's starring me in his next film. His stipulation was that my focus is wholly on my work...and him, of course."

"Of course." He had a feeling he wouldn't like this Hanover guy, but Savannah was old enough to make her own choices. "Something still confuses me about all this," he said, thinking of the past few weeks. "Why did you try to scare off my detective and make him think you were being protected by some hoods?"

"Hugo is the jealous type. If he found out that we were having this conversation, he would come unglued."

"Sounds like a healthy relationship."

"He's older. He's afraid he may be losing his virility and, therefore, me, to a younger man. I had to get rid of your private eye so I could handle things on my own timetable. Here..." She rose and went for her purse. "I have something for you."

She pulled out a thick, white envelope and handed it to him.

Wary again, Mitch asked, "What's this?"

"I'm relinquishing custody of her. There are two copies, one for each of us. Mine's already signed and notarized. On my way up here, I stopped by the concierge's desk. He told me that they have a notary who can witness your signature right away. Do me a favor and go have that done. I'll wait for you here if you don't mind. The last thing I need is someone recognizing me."

Maybe drama was the right field for Savannah, after all. But to be fair he felt an incredible relief, too. Everything he'd wanted, hoped for, was now in his grasp. He thought of Jenny and yearned to phone her this second with the news. Soon, though, he promised himself. Soon.

He snatched up his jacket. "I'll be right back," he said, heading for the door.

Jenny hummed as she entered the kitchen. "I'm home!"

"What on earth do you have there?" her grandmother asked, turning from the sink. In her hand she held the kettle for afternoon tea.

"The newest version of the rubber ducky. Isn't it adorable?"

"A bit large, I'd say. Which one of you is it for?"

"One of these days I'm going to sign you up for amateur night at a comedy club, Gran. See if I don't." Detouring to kiss her on the cheek to assure her that she didn't mind the teasing one bit, Jenny added, "Put enough water on for me, too. I could use a cup. How's the baby?"

"Fine. I don't know about her father, though. Did he say something about a schedule change to you?"

Jenny paused midway to the table. "Why?"

"He phoned a few minutes ago. He gave me a number but said he had to go out and that he would call you back."

"Let me see." She put the package on the counter by the phone and looked up at the message board. "That's a California area code. I recognize it from a number he's given me before. Oh, no! Don't tell me something's going to delay him." She reached for the phone.

"Hold on there! He said he would call *you* back!" her grandmother declared.

"Maybe I'll catch him as he's coming in. I'd like to know what's going on before I start dinner and end up ruining everything."

She punched in the numbers. Seconds later, after only one ring, a man answered. Hearing the hotel name sent Jenny's heart dropping like a battleship anchor. "Mitchell McCord's room, please," she said, wondering what could have gone wrong to make him register in a hotel. He was supposed to be on his way home! Of course, she reminded herself, as long as he was all right, nothing else mat—

"Hello?"

The female voice threw her off for an instant. Had she been connected to the wrong room? "Excuse me," she said, feeling a bit awkward. "I'm trying to get— Is Mitch McCord there?"

The woman hesitated. "This is his room, but . . . he's unavailable at the moment. Can I take a message?"

Unavailable! Whether she wanted them to or not, a number of images flashed before her mind's eye.

"Who is this?" she demanded.

"Who's *this?*" the woman replied with an even haughtier tone to her voice.

Jenny froze. She knew that voice, had heard far too many commercials not to recognize its distinct intonation.

Oh, God. "Savannah," she whispered.

Chapter Ten

"I've got it," Mitch said as he let himself into his room. He could barely restrain his enthusiasm, now that the full impact and meaning of the documents had begun to set in. It took something like Savannah's troubled expression, as she stood by the telephone, to check his euphoria.

"Good," she murmured, crossing to get her purse and sunglasses. "That's good."

"What's wrong?"

At first it didn't look as if she was going to tell him. She bit her lower lip and her gaze kept shifting back to the phone. Finally, with a sigh she said, "Who did you tell about me?"

Mitch wasn't sure what she was driving at. "You mean, about that night?"

"Whatever. Who, besides that detective, knows you and I have a history?"

"Jenny." The expression on her face had him glancing at the phone, too. "Why?"

"I think that was her just now."

"She called?"

"A woman called. She said my name and hung up." Savannah lifted a finely plucked eyebrow. "It seems as if I've created another complication for you."

She could say that again. Mitch almost groaned as he thought of what Jenny must be thinking. Damn, why hadn't she waited for him to call her as he'd asked?

"Jenny." He sighed.

"You're in love with her."

It wasn't a question and Mitch didn't have to do any deep soul-searching for an answer. "Yeah. She's been my neighbor since we were kids, and she's been an angel with Mary. She's too darned good for me, but I'm tired of trying to be noble and let some decent guy have a chance with her."

Savannah's expression turned skeptical. "Don't sell yourself short. You're decent enough." She gestured toward the phone. "Is there anything I can do to smooth things out?"

"I'll call her right back. It'll be all right." He handed her a copy of the release. "I really appreciate this, Savannah. And I hope you get everything you're looking for."

"I will." She studied him for a long moment before leaning forward and kissing his cheek. "Have a good life, Mitch."

As soon as he shut the door behind her, he lunged for the phone and dialed Jenny's number from memory. He cleared his throat on the first ring. On the second, he sat down and ran his damp palm along his thigh. By the fifth ring he had to stand again.

After eight rings, he hung up and dialed Jenny's business number. If she was there, she wouldn't fail to answer it, or else her answering machine would pick up. On the third ring, the machine began its tape. Then it cut off and he was left with dead air.

He couldn't believe it. Convinced something must have malfunctioned, he dialed again and got a busy signal.

No accident, pal. She's taken the phone off the hook.

He dialed the first number again. Now that one had a busy signal, too.

"Damn," he groaned, hanging up and burying his head in his hands. "What have you done, McCord?"

"Don't tell me, I don't want to know." Jenny's grandmother turned away from the oddly positioned phone when Jenny returned from the office where she'd just taken care of the second line.

"Fine. I won't." Jenny didn't want to talk anyway. She was too hurt, too *furious* to speak intelligently.

Of course, her grandmother didn't mean what she'd said. Jenny knew that as soon as she signaled she'd changed her mind about the tea and reached for the bottle of wine chilling in the refrigerator.

"All right, tell me."

The neck of the bottle had a heavy foil wrapper and the cork looked as if it needed a neurosurgeon to remove it. Jenny all but ripped the drawers out of the cabinets looking for the bottle opener.

"What? You're going to punish me, too?"

That reached her, and the fight went out of Jenny as if she'd just inadvertently hit the vacuum button. She slumped against the counter.

"Gran...he's in a hotel room with another woman!"

"Not just any woman. Savannah."

There was no doubt about the mockery in her grandmother's voice. It was gentle. Her ancient eyes held a life full of wisdom and compassion. But the rebuke was there nonetheless.

"You think I'm overreacting. You think I should let him explain."

"Certainly not. It's written in granite somewhere that men are a subspecies. I think we should draw and quarter him the minute he gets home, and in the years to come we'll tell his baby girl and everyone else who's interested that he was abducted by aliens."

Jenny resumed her search for the opener. Finding it, she slammed the drawer shut with enough velocity that she knew it would leave a bruise on her hip and made her belatedly worry about waking Mary. When no cry from the next room sounded, she exhaled and proceeded to open the bottle.

"You don't get it. Hearing her voice—"

"You're so sure it was her?"

"Gran. Remember the year you took me to the state fair in Dallas and walked me through the livestock pavilion? Remember that heifer that chose the worst possible moments to realize 'I am woman hear me roar'? Well, Savannah is about that difficult to forget."

"All right, so it was her. Does that mean there is no explanation?"

"I know there's an explanation. He's never stopped his own search. He didn't let a third party, an attorney, handle things for him, and this is the result."

"I suppose this means you don't want tea?" At Jenny's dark look, her grandmother busied herself with pouring out the extra water and choosing a mug.

For her part, Jenny, inexperienced in wine opening, broke an already short nail in getting the protective covering off the neck, and then shredded the cork. By the time she poured herself a glass of the Chardonnay, the contents of her glass looked as if she'd been sitting beneath a bug light for an hour.

"Does it taste as bad as it looks?" her grandmother asked, after Jenny took the first, then second sip.

"Not if you drink around the flotilla."

Her grandmother stared down into her mug and dunked the tea bag up and down. "I think we should talk."

"There's nothing to say. As a matter of fact, you should be thrilled. You were right. *I* was wrong. Mr. Friendly Skies is alive and well and having a lovely lay-over in L.A. while I take care of his *love child.*"

"You could be right."

"You bet."

"Or you could be desperately wrong."

A mustard seed-size speck of cork lodged in her throat. Although she gagged until she must have turned two shades of blue, Jenny would have swallowed a whole case of Chardonnay corks before admitting it was anything more than getting wine in the wrong pipe. "Don't you think it's time I take off those rose-colored glasses you were talking about? Okay... so I thought trust and good intentions were all that's needed to prove a point. So I believed that in the end, he would finally see me for who I am, l-love me. Hey, I'm more than willing to say, I've got the picture now."

"Yes, but since when am I the one who argues for reason and patience and you're the one who jumps to conclusions?"

Good question. But Jenny had a good answer. "Since I realized that I'm tired, Gran. I'm twenty-seven years old, and I'll grant you that's nothing in this day and age for a single woman to worry about, but considering how long I've invested being nuts about one guy, it's crippling."

Her grandmother nodded. "Then I won't say anything more. I won't even try to hug you, because I know how sensitive you are when you get this way."

"And don't put those phones back on, either."

"I wouldn't think of it. But I am cooking dinner for us. And then you're going to have a lovely long bath and relax."

"I just want to curl into a knot in my room and be alone, Gran."

Although her grandmother agreed, the baby roused and uttered one brief whimper in her usual good-natured way to announce she was ready for attention.

"Later," Jenny said with a sigh as she put the glass down. "Right now I have commitments."

He landed in Dallas at the last moments of sunset. A miracle by any way he calculated it, considering the calls, negotiations and pleas he'd gone through to achieve the feat. And by the time Mitch was heading for New Hope, his stomach was burning as if he had *two* ulcers growing there.

When he pulled into his driveway, he half expected to see Jenny's place pitch-dark and the doors boarded against him. He was almost relieved to see Fiona pluck off the day's tired and wilting flowers and sweep off the steps and walkway.

Leaving his things in the car, save the armful of flowers and the fluffy white teddy bear he'd snatched up upon his arrival at the terminal, he took long, determined strides across the lawn. "Fiona."

She raised the broom like a sentry's lance across her body. But her wise, round face held surprising satisfaction. "Well, well. You made good time."

At his approach, she shifted to where her back was to the floodlights, so he lost the ability to tell her true mood. However, he was sure of at least a bit of sarcasm in her voice. Did that mean she was going to fight him when he tried to get inside? He hoped not. He'd come here to mend their relationship, not to tear them completely apart.

"I got here as fast as I could."

"To apologize?"

"No, ma'am." At least not about what she thought. "To explain. Two different things."

Fiona remained silent for a moment, as if debating his words, and not caring whether he liked it or not. "She's upset, Mitchell. Do you think she has a right to be?"

"Yes . . . and no. I think I can make her understand. Is she inside with the baby?"

Once again Fiona hesitated. Finally, she tipped her head toward the door. "Upstairs. Second door on your left. Don't you tell her I told you. I have my reputation to protect."

He grinned, beginning to feel some of the tension inside him relax. On impulse he tugged a rose out of the bouquet and offered it to her. "Here. I'll keep her busy so she doesn't notice that one is missing," he said, and added a kiss on her cheek for good measure.

As he started up the steps, he got a swat on his butt. "Hey!"

"That's for scaring the pink out of my hair and my little girl's cheeks!" she snapped, pointing the rose at him. But just as quickly a twinkle came into her eyes. "Go on now. You've kept her waiting long enough!"

He figured that if he spent the rest of his life trying, he would never figure out women. He did, however, have a hunch that he would find the attempt entertaining, especially since he would be outnumbered. For a while, he amended with a secret grin.

Inside he moved faster, taking the stairs two at a time. He heard the water splashing before he reached the top, and thought she must be elbow deep in giving the baby a bath.

She was that, all right. And more.

When he pushed open the slightly ajar door, he saw a sight he swore he would cherish the rest of his life. There she was with her sable hair piled high on her head and dressed only in bubbles. Cradled in her lap and arms, his child cooed contentedly. The two of them had been watching a huge white duck and several ducklings swim in and out of foamy mountains. Then they spotted him.

She gasped.

He sighed.

Mary gurgled and slapped and kicked at the water.

"You two are the most beautiful sight I've ever seen," he murmured, wishing he had a camera.

"Oh! You ... get out!"

Because he'd anticipated a chilly reception at first, he found it easier to ignore her curt command. He even managed a calm smile as he stepped inside and crouched beside the tub. "Brought you both a little peace offering," he said, holding up the roses and the bear.

Her lower lip came out slightly, making her look adorably petulant. "That's not going to work, Mc-Cord."

That's not what his daughter was indicating. Mitch barely suppressed a chuckle, because Mary's eyes grew round and eager as she focused on the fluffy toy. While he made it dance on the tub's edge to entertain her, he let his gaze wander over Jenny's flushed face, the damp curls threatening to tumble from her casual but sexy upswept hairdo.

"Sweetheart, I got back as soon as I could swap out flights with one of the guys."

"You needn't have bothered. I would have been happy to care for Mary overnight. Now, please, go away."

Although she averted her face, and Mitch knew she would try to block him out, he had to keep talking. He soothed the crack in his confidence by taking in the elegant length of her neck, her exquisite shoulders, the alluring swell of her breasts—although more of them were hidden by bubbles than he cared for.

"Not yet. You have to listen to me first."

"*Have* to?"

"Jen...this afternoon the plane experienced mechanical problems." She whipped around and stared at him. "It's all right, we got down safely, but they couldn't get things to where they would let us take the plane up this afternoon."

"You were in danger and you're only telling me *now?*"

Danger to him was relative. He figured he could get out of bed one morning and have his house explode from a faulty gas line or something. When it was his time, it was his time. "There was no reason to get you upset. We managed just fine. But the plane wasn't coming back today and so they wanted us to lay over until tomorrow. As usual, when a situation calls for us to lay over, we checked into the airport hotel.''

Jenny's eyes turned opaque with pain. ''Yes, and when I called your room, I got Savannah.''

''She followed me to the hotel. I suppose she phoned the main office to find out when I would be in town. It's not all that difficult to figure out.''

''I'm only interested in why she was there at all.''

It pleased him to hear she wanted answers. A moment ago she didn't want to talk to him at all. ''She's involved in a relationship and she's concerned about her... fiancé getting jealous.''

Jenny looked skeptical. ''The hood?''

''There is no hood. That was all hype. There's just an eccentric filmmaker.''

''Oh, for pity's sake!'' Jenny's look said she didn't know whether to believe him or not. ''Look, I know you never contacted an attorney. You've been looking for her on your own. Why you felt the need to lie to me—''

''It wasn't a 'need.' I just wanted to do things my way. I was also concerned with keeping this situation as private as I could. Jen, I was thinking about Mary as much as you or us. Her future affects ours. And I don't mind saying it's all turned out better than we could have hoped.''

The baby reached for the bear, and Jenny tried to appease her with one of the ducklings. Mitch could tell she was fighting herself and losing fast.

''What do you mean?'' she asked, not quite meeting his eyes.

He reached into his inside pocket. "She had this drawn up, relinquishing all claim to Mary. That's why I wasn't there when you called. I'd raced downstairs to get the thing notarized, scared to death that the bubble would burst on the fantasy."

Her gaze lowered to the affidavit he held up for her. "Oh, my...it's real." She finally met his gaze. "And here I thought— Mitch, I was so jealous."

"I know." He grinned with unabashed delight. "I love it. But what's best of all is that this mess is over. Savannah's out of our lives and she's moving on with hers."

Jenny stiffened. "Some life."

"That doesn't matter. She did the right thing, Jen. Now Mary will really be ours."

"Yours," Jenny said, correcting him. Her expression grew embarrassed and shy again, the way it had when he'd first walked into the bathroom.

Mitch shook his head and touched her cheek with the roses. With her looking like a fantasy herself, he could prolong this all night if that's the way she wanted to play it—as long as he got what he wanted in the end. Her.

"You want to know the greatest thing of all?" he asked, noting that the outer rims of the roses matched the color of her moist lips.

"You're going to be best man at her wedding?"

"Mary's name is really Mary."

Jenny tightened her arms around the baby. "What?"

"Shawna—Savannah's variation of my Sean—Mary McCord."

"Oh, my. Fate *does* work in mysterious ways."

"That's what I thought. And that's why I couldn't wait to call and tell you the good news. Because it meant

that now I was free to concentrate on us . . . the way I
realize I've wanted to for a long time."

Color bloomed in Jenny's cheeks all over again.
"You don't have to say that, Mitch."

"What else should a man who's crazy in love say?"

Her eyes went wide. Her lips parted, but not a word
came out.

"Finally have you speechless, I see."

She had to swallow to force out, "It would seem so."

"I love you, Jen. We may have to spend our first
Christmas apart because of the IOUs I gave to get home
tonight, but it'll be worth it if you tell me that you'll
marry me and be Mary's mommy." When she still
didn't reply, he cocked his head. "Sweetheart? You
better say something fast, or I'm going to have to climb
into that tub and shock you into answering."

"Kiss me. Kiss me and maybe then I'll know this is
really happening."

"I thought you'd never ask."

He fastened his mouth to hers, thinking there were
some emotions they shared that would always tran-
scend words. He proved it when within seconds he had
her moaning softly. Within a few more she was linking
her free arm around his neck and pulling him closer.

Dear heaven, the hours apart and the day's pressures
had taken their toll, he thought, discovering he was
shaking as if he were in the midst of his own personal
earthquake. Blindly placing the flowers and bear on the
floor beside him, he sank onto his knees, framed Jenny's face with his hands and deepened the kiss even
more . . . until his heart was pounding so hard the pressure threatened to squeeze tears from around his tightly
shut eyes . . . until he was one second away from lifting

her and the baby out of the tub so he could hold them both closer to the sweet ache in his heart.

Suddenly there was a loud gurgle and a slap of water. He and Jenny broke apart as bubbles and water drenched them. Looking delighted with herself, Mary kicked the water again.

"Little..."

"Mary!"

Mitch burst into laughter, but had to wipe bubbles off his mustache. "I take it that you're giving us your blessing, young lady?" When she gurgled again, he planted a kiss on her cheek—and before straightening, added another on Jenny's breast just above an evaporating cloud of bubbles. It was delicious to feel her pulse quicken and see her eyes shimmer with invitation and dreams.

"Now say what you've been showing me for ages," he whispered gruffly, brushing a strand of her hair behind her ear. "You have to, you know. Your grandmother approves. Oh, she tries to pretend she doesn't, but I finally figured it out tonight. She likes me. She just can't stop playing devil's advocate."

"I know. We'll have to cure her. Together."

"Good idea." He smiled and focused on her mouth. "Well?"

"I love you, McCord. With all my heart."

"Thank God," he mouthed, seeking her lips again.

Then there was another long kiss... and yet another.

Finally he held a large bath towel for his two beauties, whom he helped to stand, only so he could pull them close to his heart.

"Let's make this a short engagement. Please?" he whispered to Jenny as the bathwater from her body soaked through his uniform and steamed against his body.

"Very short," Jenny whispered into his mouth.

Between them, Mary clasped her hands together and cooed.

It was the sweetest unanimous agreement Mitch had ever heard.

* * * * *

*Don't miss the next book
in Silhouette's exciting
DADDY KNOWS LAST series.*

Here's a sneak preview of

MARRIED . . . WITH TWINS!

*by Jennifer Mikels
available in September from
Silhouette Special Edition*

Married . . . with Twins!

"You're a daddy now," someone had said to him. He couldn't even remember who'd said the words. He'd been reeling from the shock. Unlike other men who had nine months to prepare for fatherhood, Lucas Kincaid had become a daddy overnight.

Fate threw some real curves, he decided. Just as he and his wife were on the verge of divorce, they'd become guardians of twin two-year-olds. Disbelief still shadowing him, he cradled a Victorian dollhouse in his arms and turned toward the back door of the bi-level house he and Val had bought four years ago.

From the kitchen, ear-piercing screams drifted to him. Urchins with blond ponytails, pug noses and quick grins, Brooke and Traci Dawson had kept Val and him on their toes since seven this morning.

Luke sidestepped two tricycles and nearly kicked over Val's clay pot filled with geraniums. He'd always wanted children. He knew a lot of men could care less, but of all the patients he saw, he liked the kids best. They asked the most absurd questions, they lightened his day, they made him remember why he'd decided on a career in medicine.

Nearing the back door, he shifted the dollhouse to one arm and reached to open the screen door. His gaze went to his wife. A small, slender woman with long legs and hair the color of deep rich coffee, she had the lithe figure of an athlete or a dancer. Her dark brown eyes were wide and expressive, her face animated as she talked low to the twins. In her hand was the object of battle, a Raggedy Ann doll.

Pouting two-year-olds glared up at her until she stretched and grabbed two cookies from an opened package on the counter. Traci's pout lifted first. She crawled onto Val's lap and curled an arm around her neck. More interested in the cookie than affection, Brooke plopped on the floor to munch away.

At the slam of the screen door behind him, Val angled a look over her shoulder in his direction. Out of necessity, they'd spent more time together this morning than they had in weeks. "Where is this going?" he asked about the dollhouse.

"A good question," she said, actually sounding a little amused. "Your den," she finally answered and shrugged.

That wasn't the response he'd expected, but he didn't protest. Though she was usually organized, Valerie looked a bit overwhelmed at the moment. Luke sensed she had no idea where to put anything except the twins' clothes.

"Hi, lion," Brooke sang out as Val lifted a fuzzy tan one from a carton of stuffed animals. All morning she'd greeted everything that had been unpacked. As Luke inched his way around the child, her blond head swiveled toward him. "Lu-cas, don't drop."

Amusement rippled through him. He'd had his share of toddlers in his office, but their tendency toward bossiness had eluded him until this up-close and personal encounter. Crossing the living room, he felt resistance on his leg.

"Can me help?" Brooke asked, yanking on his jeans.

Traci suddenly tugged on the other leg. "No." Her blond ponytail swung with the wag of her head. "Traci help."

As Brooke's fingers tightened on the denim, Luke contemplated another battle. But never more than a step behind the girls, Val predictably popped around the kitchen doorway, her arms hugging stuffed animals.

Was it good-humored sympathy or something else Luke read in the dark gaze smiling at him?

Letting the stuffed animals tumble from her arms onto the living room carpet, Valerie flashed a quick, amused smile. It tore at him. For months, he'd yearned to see her like this. Instead, sorrow had haunted her eyes.

"Girls, I need help," she said, offering a hand to each twin.

With no hesitation, Brooke bounded to her. "Me do it."

Just as eager, Traci trailed. "Traci do it."

"Round three," Luke said on a chuckle.

Val looked at her husband. For an instant, she could almost remember the way they used to be. When they'd met, she'd thought he was the perfect one for her. With his tall, rangy build, dark hair and chiseled features, he'd garnered his share of women, but her feelings had gone beyond his good looks. Personable and intelligent, he'd been easy to talk to, easy to laugh with, and wonderful to make love with.

Until last February, when their world had screeched to a halt.

There had been months since that night when they couldn't be around each other, couldn't stand to see each other's eyes and the sadness that mirrored their own. She'd withdrawn into herself; he'd drifted away from her. They'd stopped talking and laughing. They'd stopped making love. And they had faced the inevitable weeks ago—their marriage was over. But now their agreed divorce threatened a promise to friends, one that had been made when their marriage had been perfect.

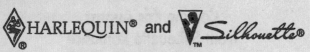

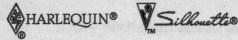 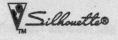

Coming this August
from Silhouette Romance

Expanding upon our popular Fabulous Fathers series, these irresistable heros are going even farther beyond daddy duty... for the love of children and unforgettable heroines!

UNDERCOVER DADDY
by
Lindsay Longford
(SR#1168, August)

Detective Walker Ford had always loved Kate McDaniels, but she'd married his best friend. Now she was widowed with an infant son—and they desperately needed his help. Walker had sworn to protect the baby with his life—but who would protect his heart from the boy's beautiful mother?

Don't miss this Super Fabulous Father—only in

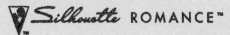

SFF896

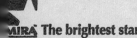

SOMETIMES BIG SURPRISES
COME IN SMALL PACKAGES!

Bundles
of Joy

THE MAN WHO WOULD BE DADDY
by
Marie Ferrarella

He'd rescued her baby! Single mom Christa Winslow couldn't
thank Malcolm Evans enough. But could this handsome hero
help mother and child once again? Christa knew her little girl
needed a father and that beneath Malcolm's gruff exterior
lay the tender soul of a man who would be daddy....

Don't miss this adorable **Bundles of Joy**,
available in September, only from

The exciting new cross-line continuity series about love, marriage—and Daddy's unexpected need for a baby carriage!

You loved

THE BABY NOTION by Dixie Browning (Desire #1011 7/96)
and
BABY IN A BASKET by Helen R. Myers
(Romance #1169 8/96)

Now the series continues with...

MARRIED...WITH TWINS! by Jennifer Mikels
(Special Edition #1054 9/96)

The soon-to-be separated Kincaids just found out they're about to be parents. Will their newfound family grant them a second chance at marriage?

Don't miss the next books in this wonderful series:

HOW TO HOOK A HUSBAND (AND A BABY)
by Carolyn Zane (Yours Truly #29 10/96)

DISCOVERED: DADDY
by Marilyn Pappano (Intimate Moments #746 11/96)

DADDY KNOWS LAST continues each month...
only from

Silhouette®

Look us up on-line at: http://www.romance.net

DKL-SE

Bestselling Author
LISA
JACKSON

Continues the twelve-book series—FORTUNE'S CHILDREN
in August 1996 with Book Two

THE MILLIONAIRE AND THE COWGIRL

When playboy millionaire Kyle Fortune inherited a Wyoming
ranch from his grandmother, he never expected to come
face-to-face with Samantha Rawlings, the willful woman
he'd never forgotten...and the daughter he'd never known.
Although Kyle enjoyed his jet-setting life-style, Samantha and
Caitlyn made him yearn for hearth and home.

MEET THE FORTUNES—a family whose legacy is greater than
riches. Because where there's a will...there's a *wedding!*

*A CASTING CALL TO
ALL FORTUNE'S CHILDREN FANS!*
If you are truly one of the fortunate
few, you may win a trip to
Los Angeles to audition for
Wheel of Fortune®. Look for
details in all retail Fortune's Children titles!

Look us up on-line at: http://www.romance.net

Waiting for you at the altar this fall...

THE BEST MEN

by
Karen Rose Smith

Marriage is meant to be for these sexy single guys...once they stand up as best men for their best friends.

"Just, 'cause I'm having a hard time raising my three little cowpokes does *not* mean I'm looking for a wife!"
—*Cade Gallagher, the hard-nosed, softhearted*
COWBOY AT THE WEDDING (SR #1171 8/96)

"I swear I didn't know she was pregnant when I left town!"
—*Gavin Bradley, the last to know, but still a*
MOST ELIGIBLE DAD (SR #1174 9/96)

"Why is everyone so shocked that I agreed to marry a total stranger?"
—*Nathan Maxwell, the surprising husband-to-be in*
A GROOM AND A PROMISE (SR #1181 10/96)

Three of the closest friends, the finest fathers—
THE BEST MEN to marry! Coming to you only in

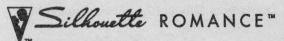

Silhouette ROMANCE™